Y0-BED-857

TIGER MOTH

THE PEST SHOW ON EARTH

Librarian Reviewer
Katharine Kan
Graphic novel reviewer and Library Consultant, Panama City, FL
MLS in Library and Information Studies, University of Hawaii at
Manoa, HI

Reading Consultant
Elizabeth Stedem
Educator/Consultant, Colorado Springs, CO
MA in Elementary Education, University of Denver, CO

STONE ARCH BOOKS
MINNEAPOLIS   SAN DIEGO

HIGHLAND PARK PUBLIC LIBRARY
494 LAUREL AVE.
HIGHLAND PARK, IL 60035-2690
847-432-0216

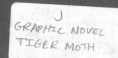

J
GRAPHIC NOVEL
TIGER MOTH

Graphic Sparks are published by Stone Arch Books
151 Good Counsel Drive, P.O. Box 669
Mankato, Minnesota 56002
www.stonearchbooks.com

Copyright © 2008 by Stone Arch Books

All rights reserved. No part of this publication may be reproduced
in whole or in part, or stored in a retrieval system, or transmitted in any
form or by any means, electronic, mechanical, photocopying, recording,
or otherwise, without written permission of the publisher.

Library of Congress Cataloging-in-Publication Data
Reynolds, Aaron, 1970–
    The Pest Show on Earth / by Aaron Reynolds; illustrated by Erik Lervold.
    p. cm. — (Graphic Sparks—Tiger Moth)
    ISBN 978-1-4342-0454-7 (library binding)
    ISBN 978-1-4342-0504-9 (paperback)
    1. Graphic novels. I. Lervold, Erik. II. Title.
PN6727.R45P47 2008
741.5'973—dc22   2007031254

Summary: When the carnival comes to town, Tiger Moth and his sidekick, Kung Pow,
let their ninja guard down. But not for long! This funfest is an evil trick by Weevil, the
world's evilest insect. Now, the fourth-grade ninja duo must stop the show before the main
attraction . . . the deadly Wing Kong!

Art Director: Heather Kindseth
Graphic Designer: Brann Garvey

1 2 3 4 5 6 13 12 11 10 09 08

Printed in the United States of America

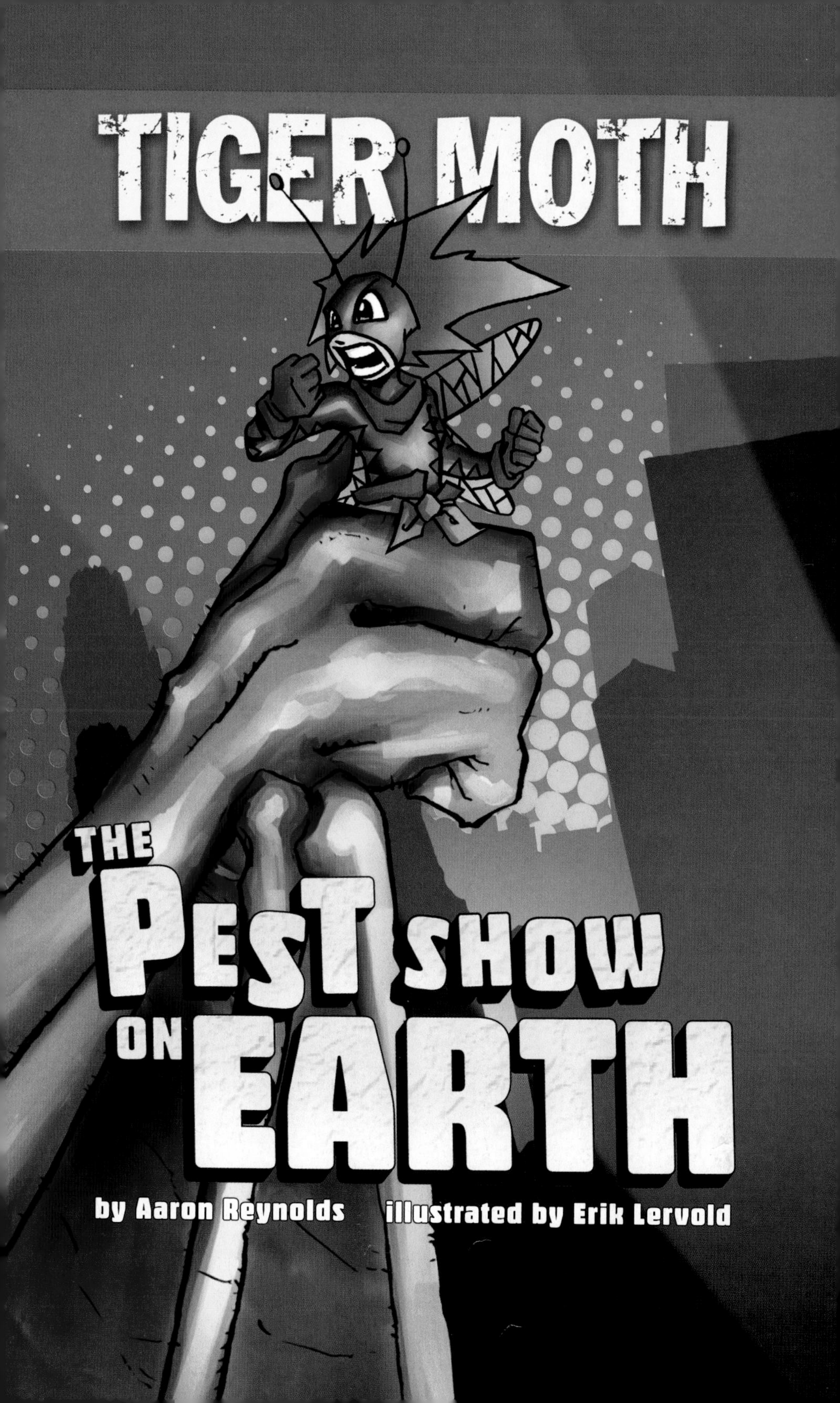
TIGER MOTH
THE PEST SHOW ON EARTH
by Aaron Reynolds
illustrated by Erik Lervold

Cast of Characters

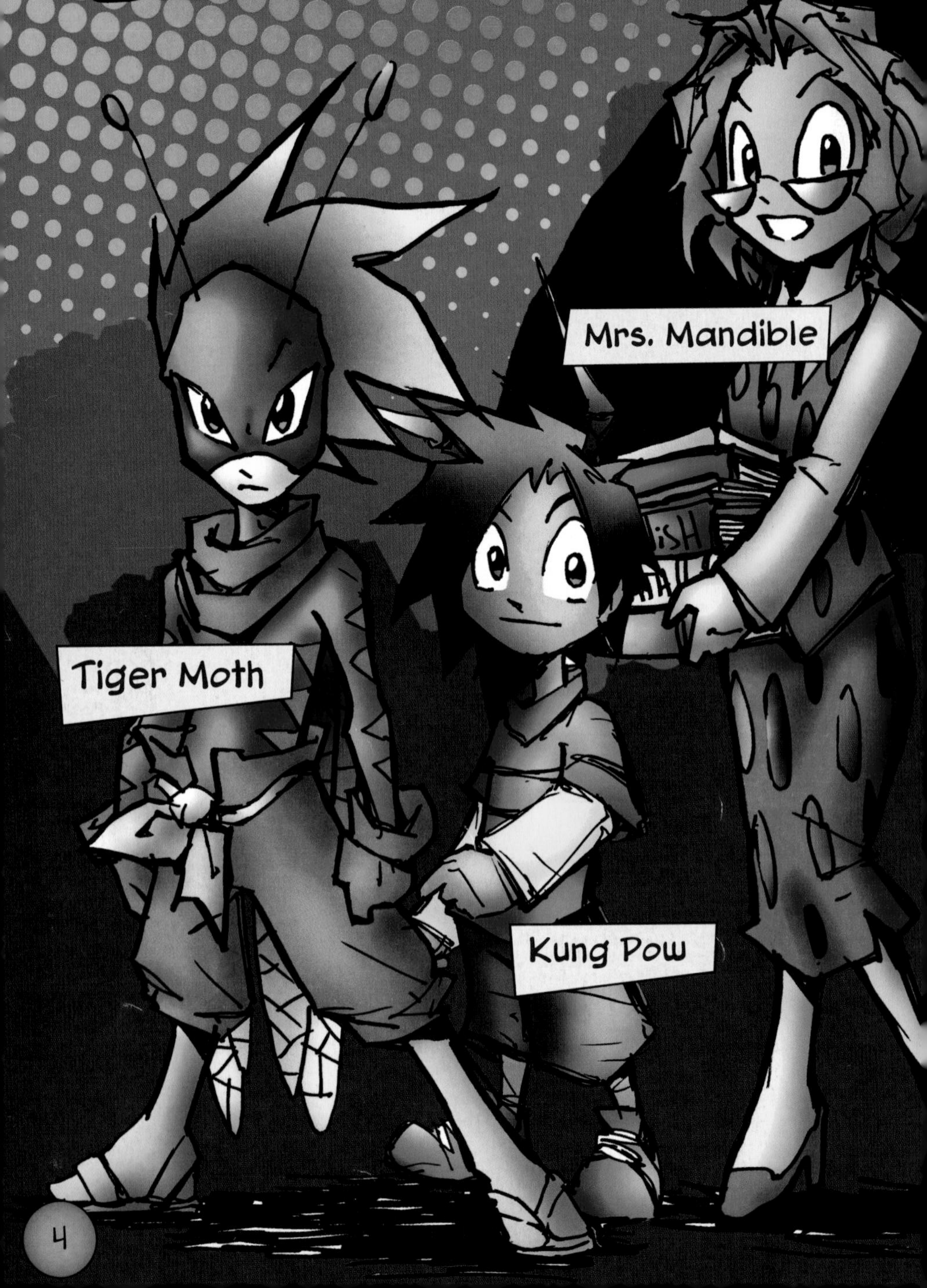
Mrs. Mandible
Tiger Moth
Kung Pow

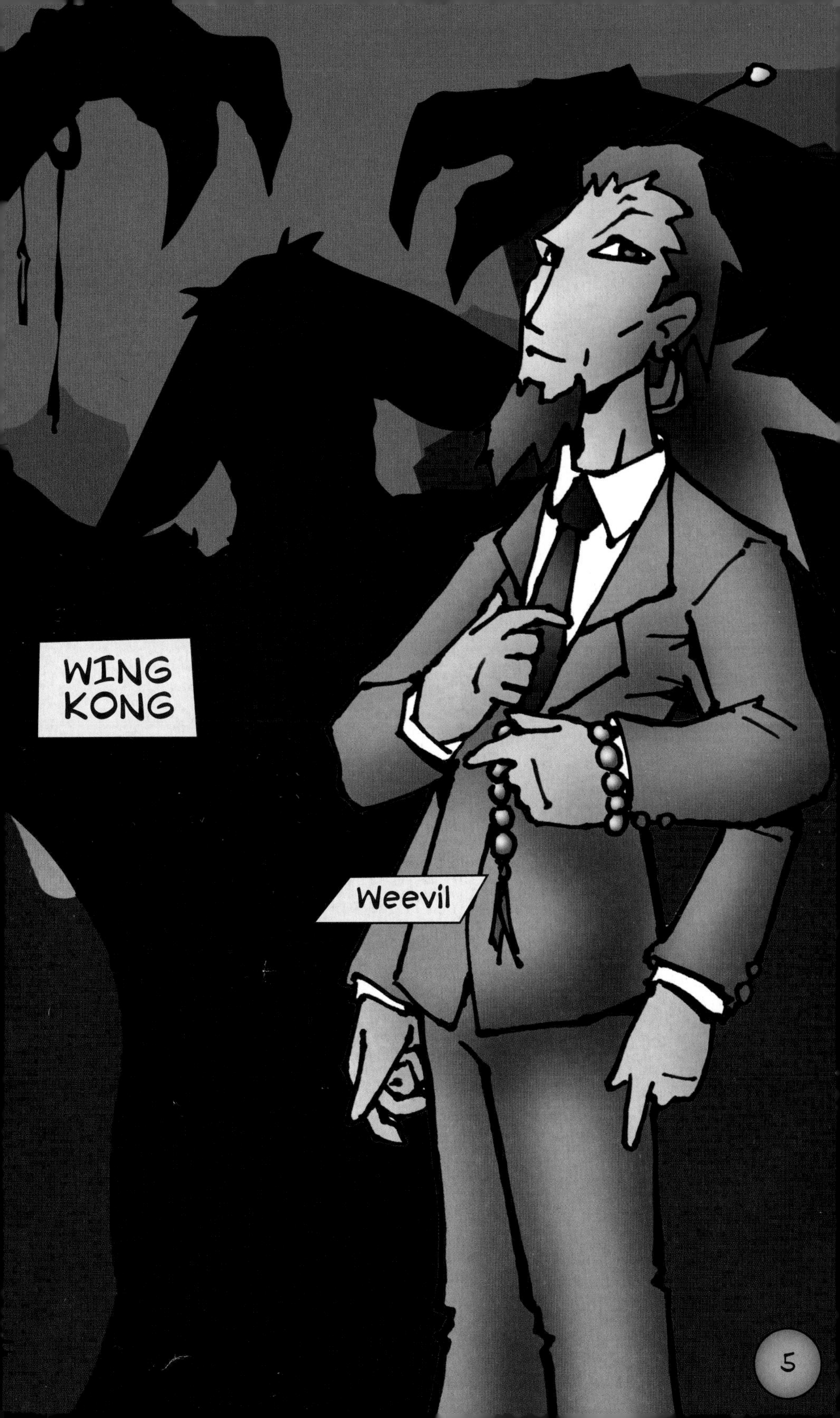
WING KONG
Weevil

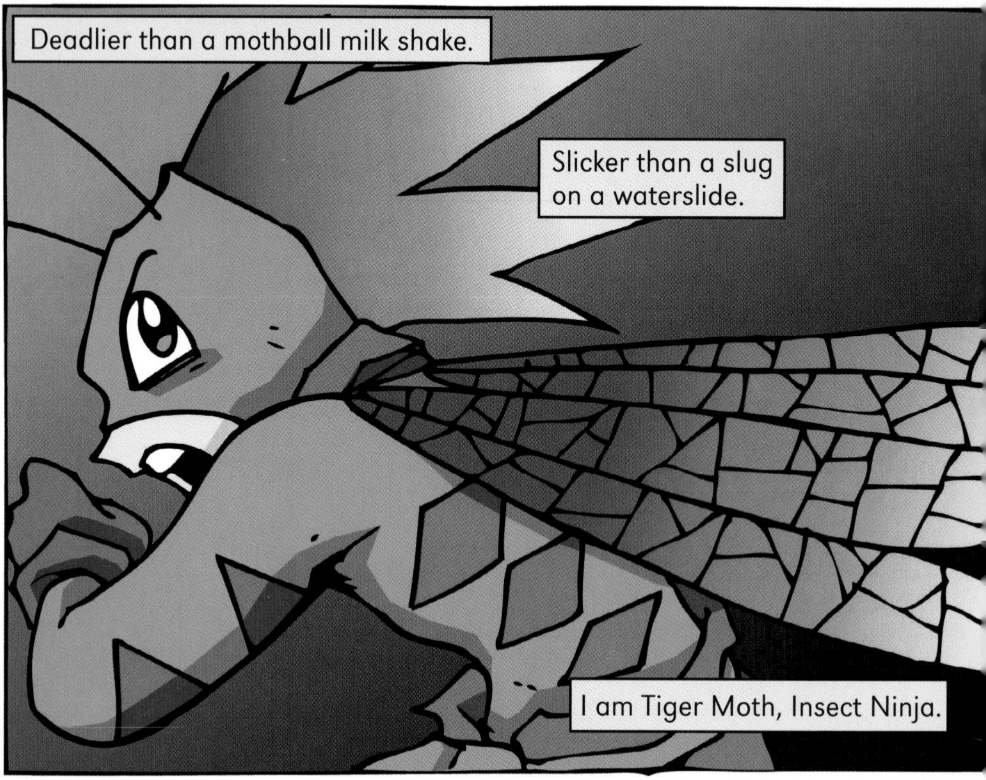
Deadlier than a mothball milk shake.
Slicker than a slug on a waterslide.
I am Tiger Moth, Insect Ninja.

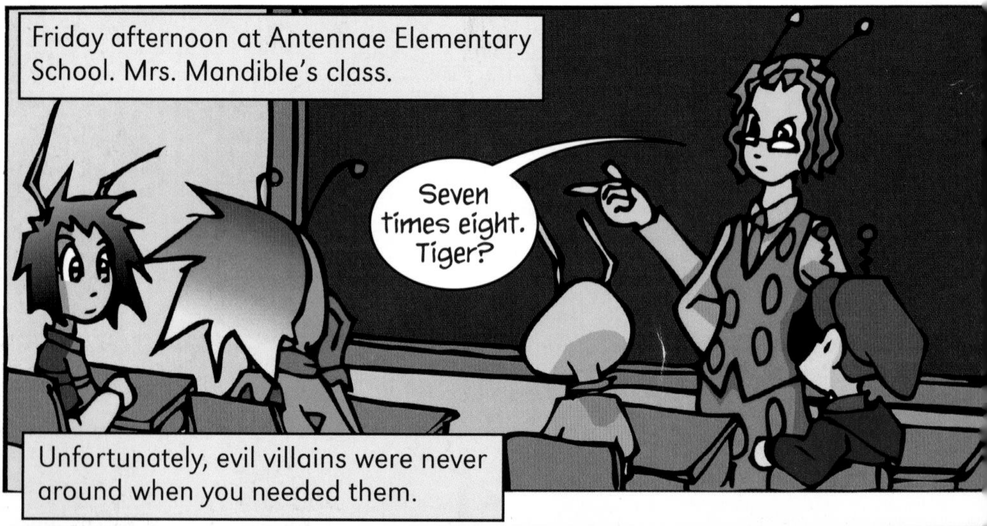
Friday afternoon at Antennae Elementary School. Mrs. Mandible's class.
Seven times eight. Tiger?
Unfortunately, evil villains were never around when you needed them.

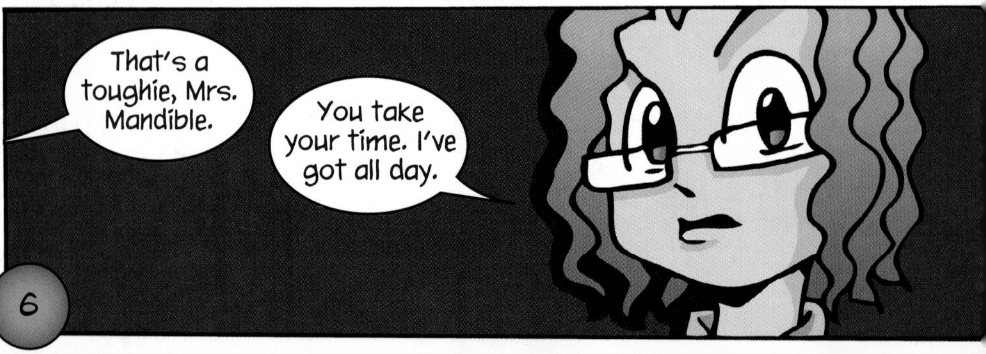
That's a toughie, Mrs. Mandible.
You take your time. I've got all day.

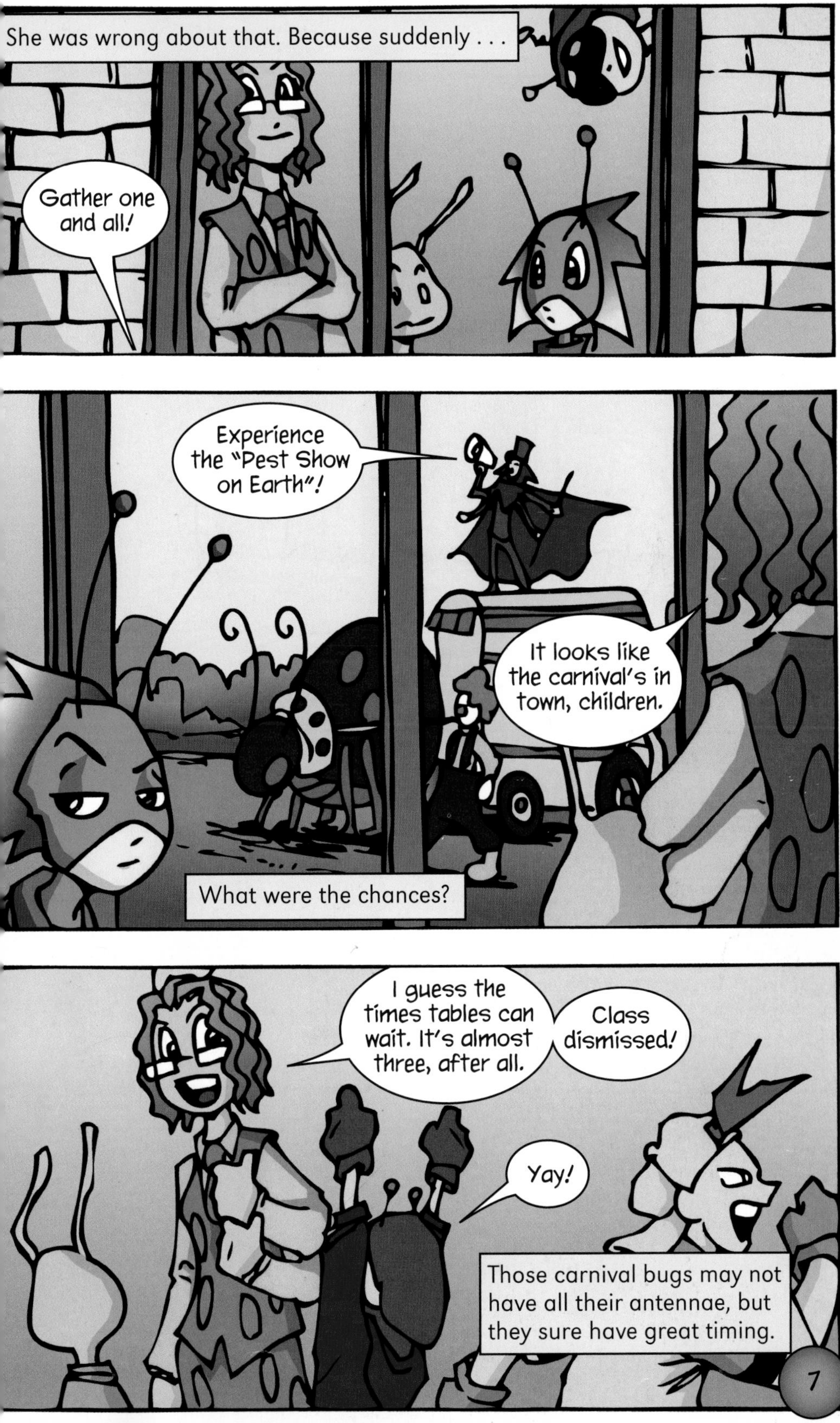

She was wrong about that. Because suddenly . . .
Gather one and all!
Experience the "Pest Show on Earth"!
It looks like the carnival's in town, children.
What were the chances?
I guess the times tables can wait. It's almost three, after all.
Class dismissed!
Yay!
Those carnival bugs may not have all their antennae, but they sure have great timing.

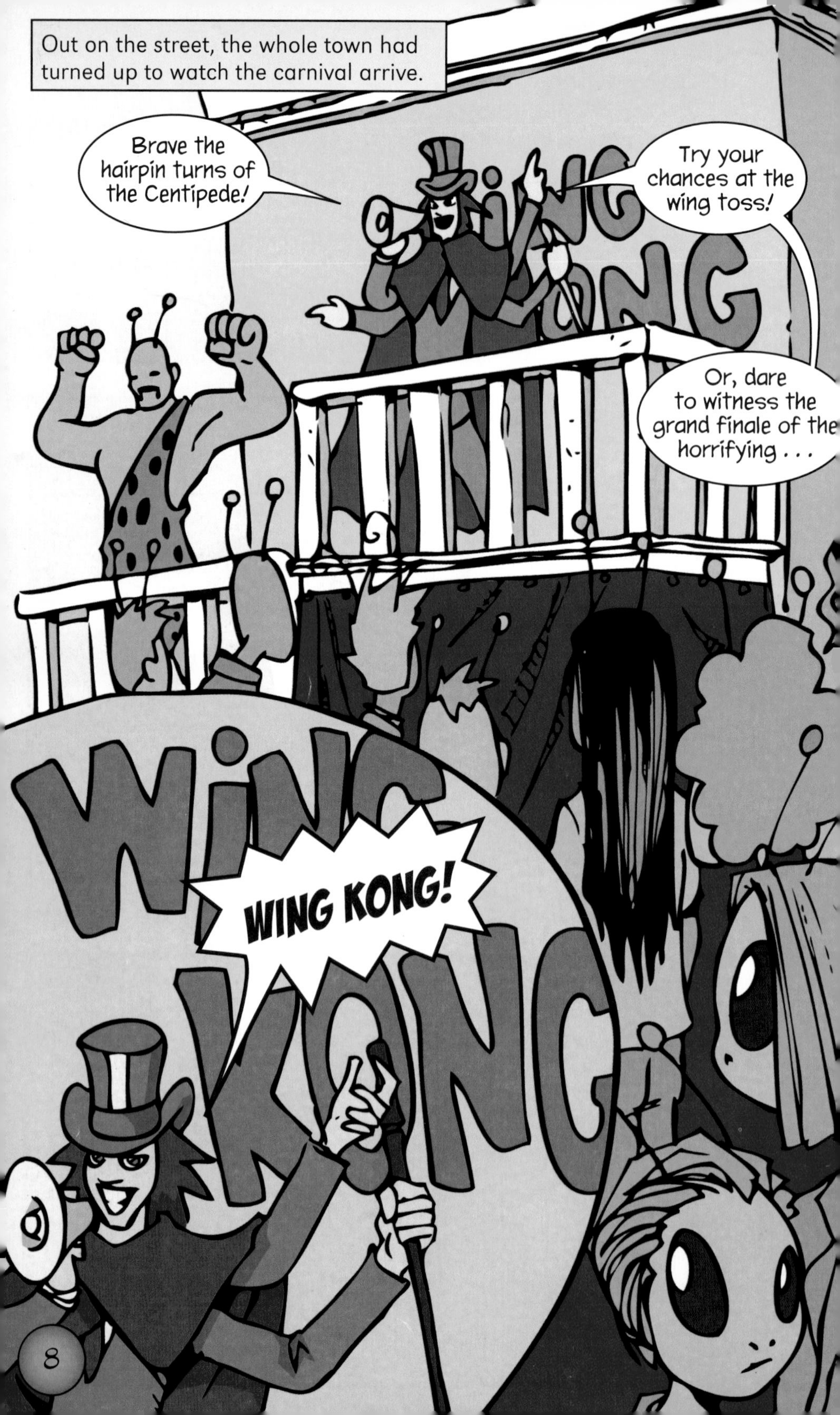
Out on the street, the whole town had turned up to watch the carnival arrive.
Brave the hairpin turns of the Centipede!
Try your chances at the wing toss!
Or, dare to witness the grand finale of the horrifying . . .
WING KONG!
WING KONG

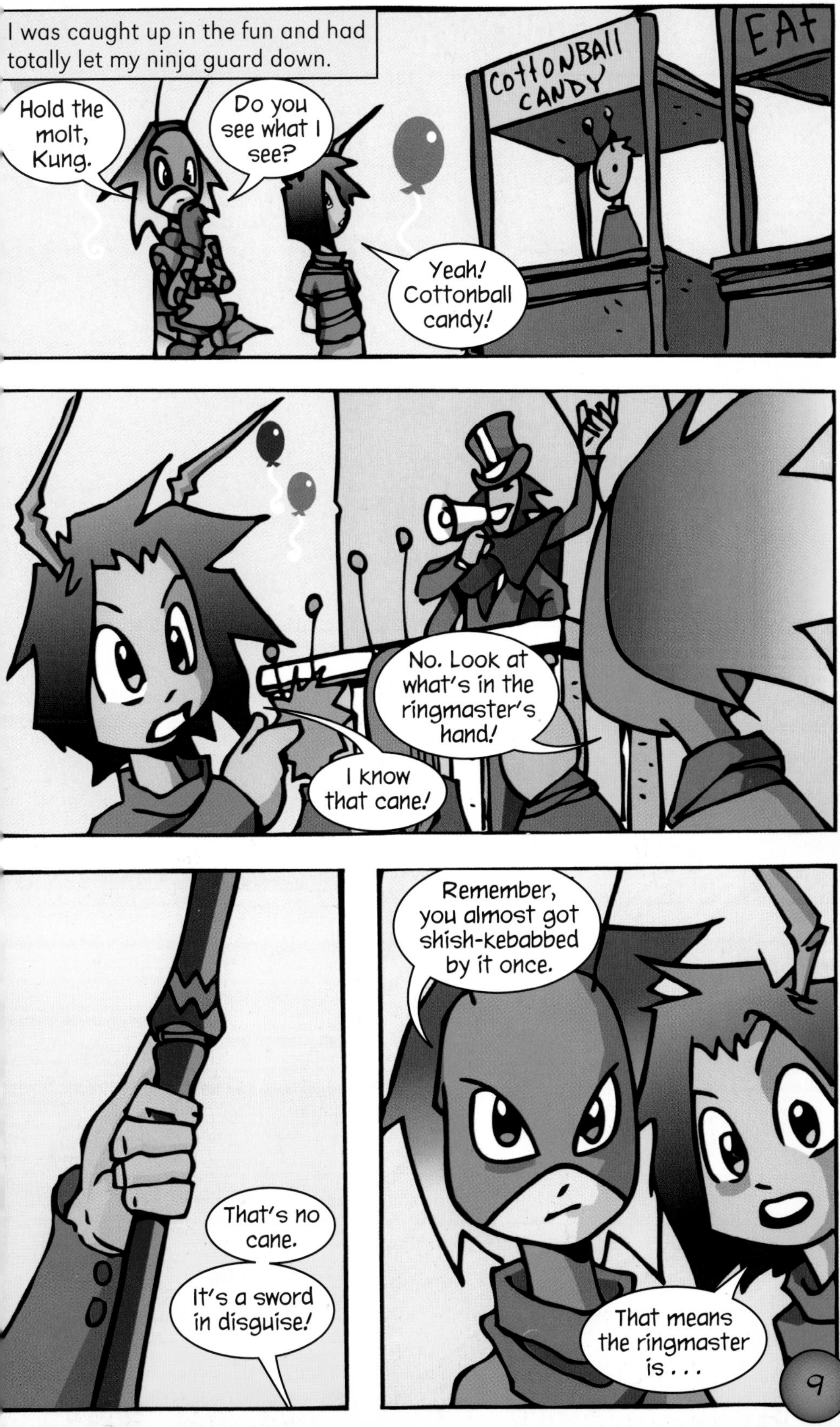
I was caught up in the fun and had totally let my ninja guard down.
Hold the molt, Kung.
Do you see what I see?
Yeah! Cottonball candy!
COTTONBALL CANDY
EAT
No. Look at what's in the ringmaster's hand!
I know that cane!
That's no cane.
It's a sword in disguise!
Remember, you almost got shish-kebabbed by it once.
That means the ringmaster is . . .

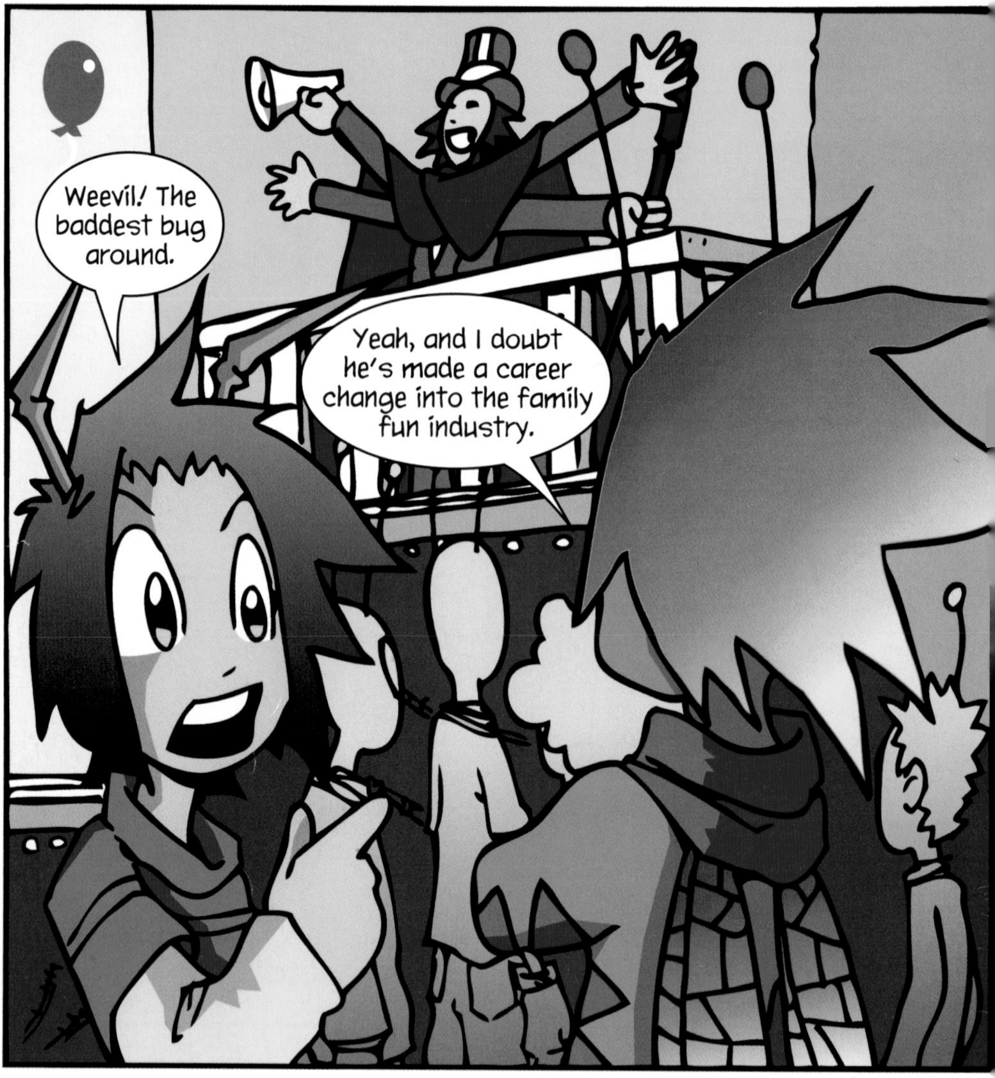
Weevil! The baddest bug around.
Yeah, and I doubt he's made a career change into the family fun industry.

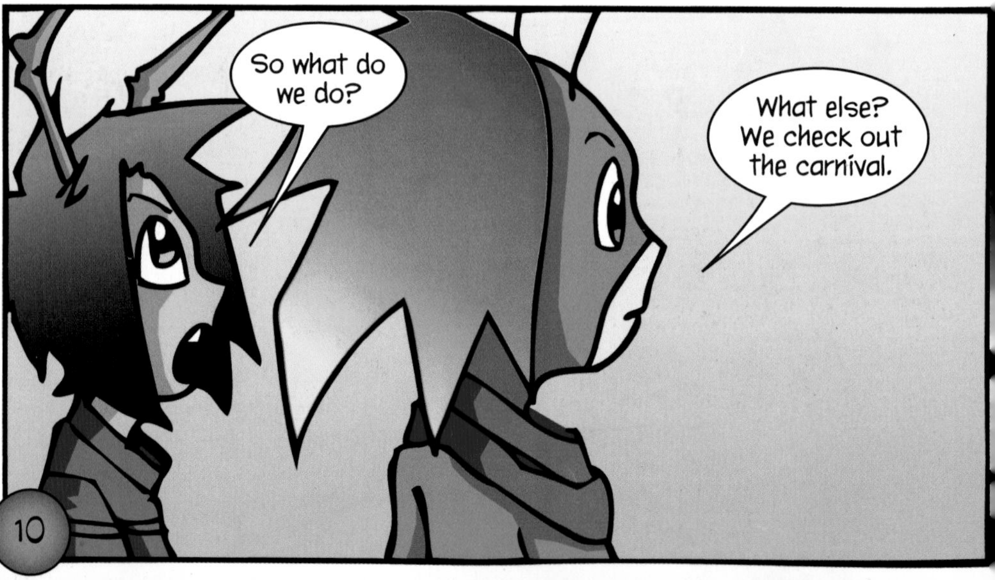
So what do we do?
What else? We check out the carnival.

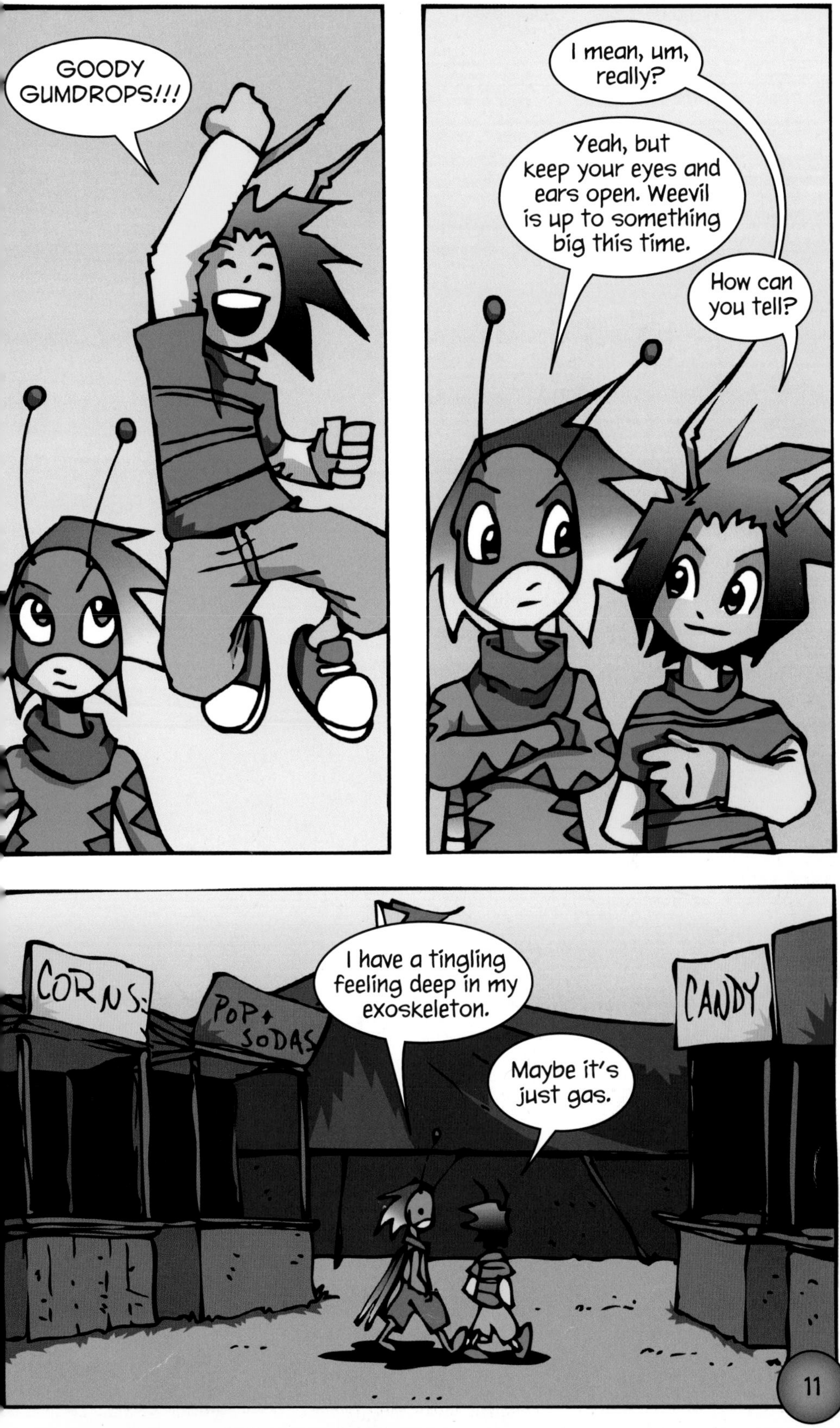
GOODY GUMDROPS!!!
I mean, um, really?
Yeah, but keep your eyes and ears open. Weevil is up to something big this time.
How can you tell?
CORNS
POP + SODAS
CANDY
I have a tingling feeling deep in my exoskeleton.
Maybe it's just gas.

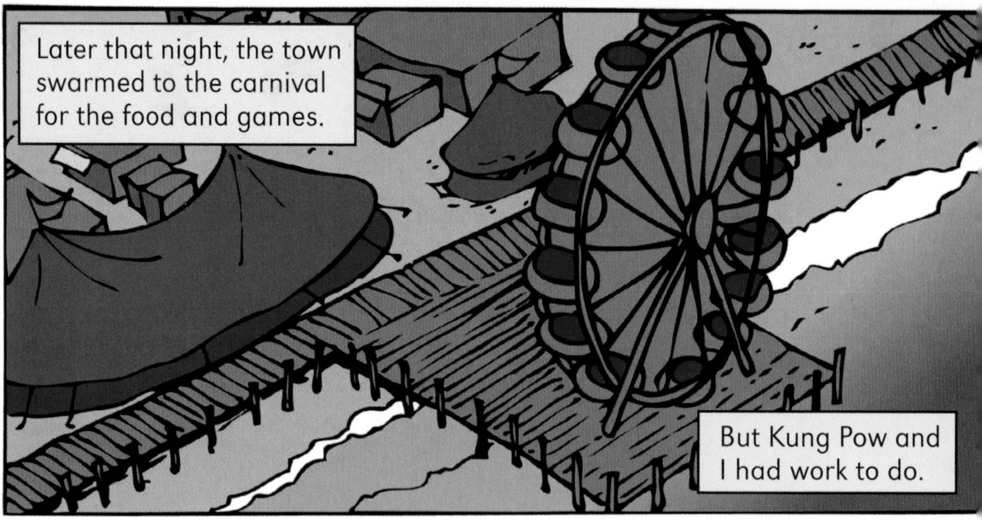
Later that night, the town swarmed to the carnival for the food and games.
But Kung Pow and I had work to do.

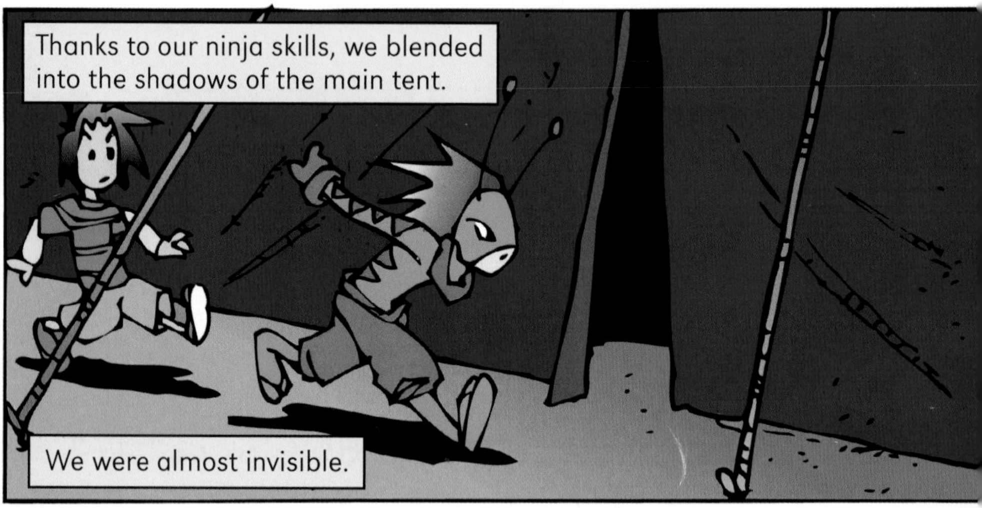
Thanks to our ninja skills, we blended into the shadows of the main tent.
We were almost invisible.

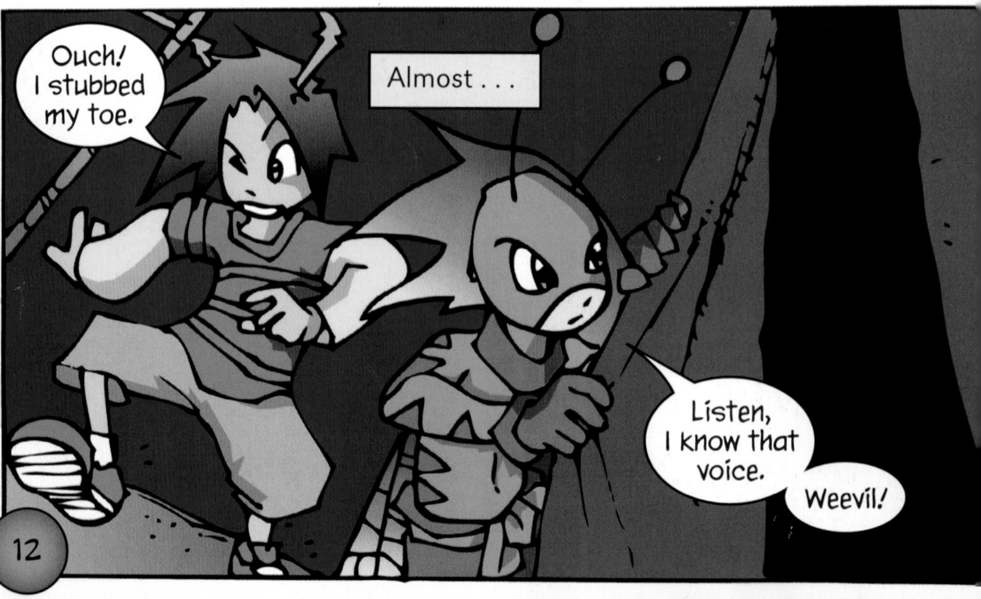
Ouch! I stubbed my toe.
Almost . . .
Listen, I know that voice.
Weevil!

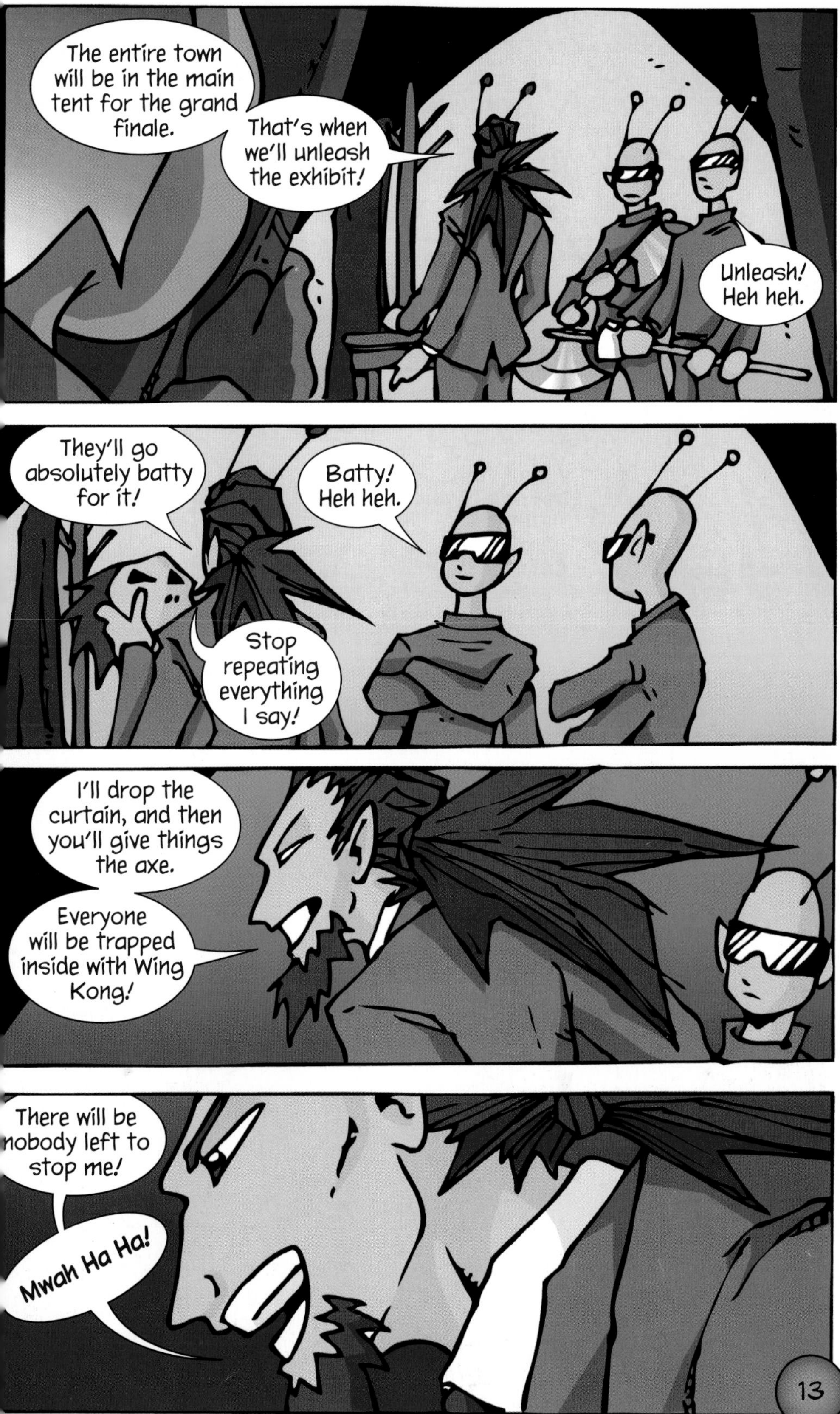
The entire town will be in the main tent for the grand finale.
That's when we'll unleash the exhibit!
Unleash! Heh heh.
They'll go absolutely batty for it!
Batty! Heh heh.
Stop repeating everything I say!
I'll drop the curtain, and then you'll give things the axe.
Everyone will be trapped inside with Wing Kong!
There will be nobody left to stop me!
Mwah Ha Ha!

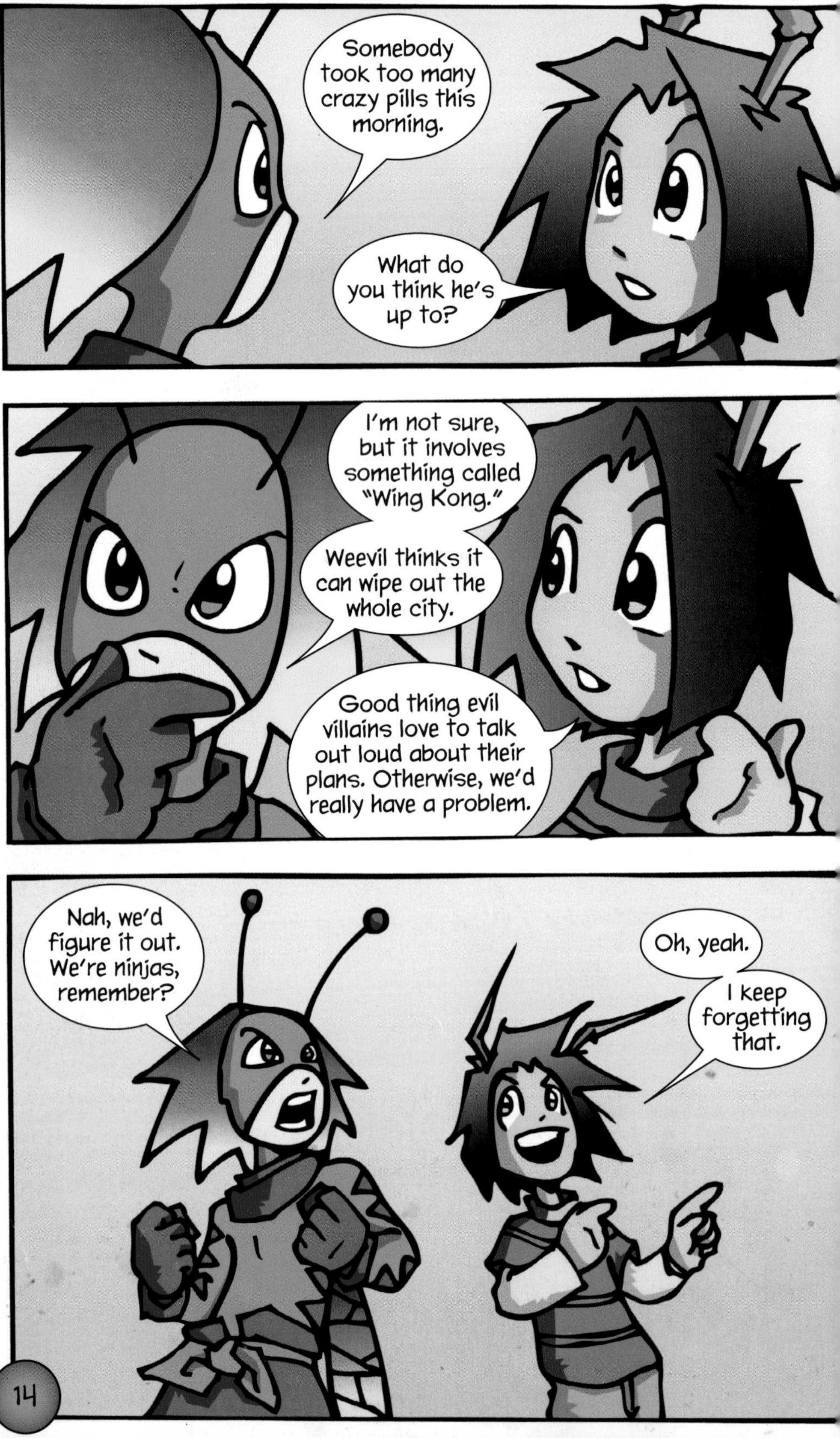
Somebody took too many crazy pills this morning.
What do you think he's up to?
I'm not sure, but it involves something called "Wing Kong."
Weevil thinks it can wipe out the whole city.
Good thing evil villains love to talk out loud about their plans. Otherwise, we'd really have a problem.
Nah, we'd figure it out. We're ninjas, remember?
Oh, yeah.
I keep forgetting that.

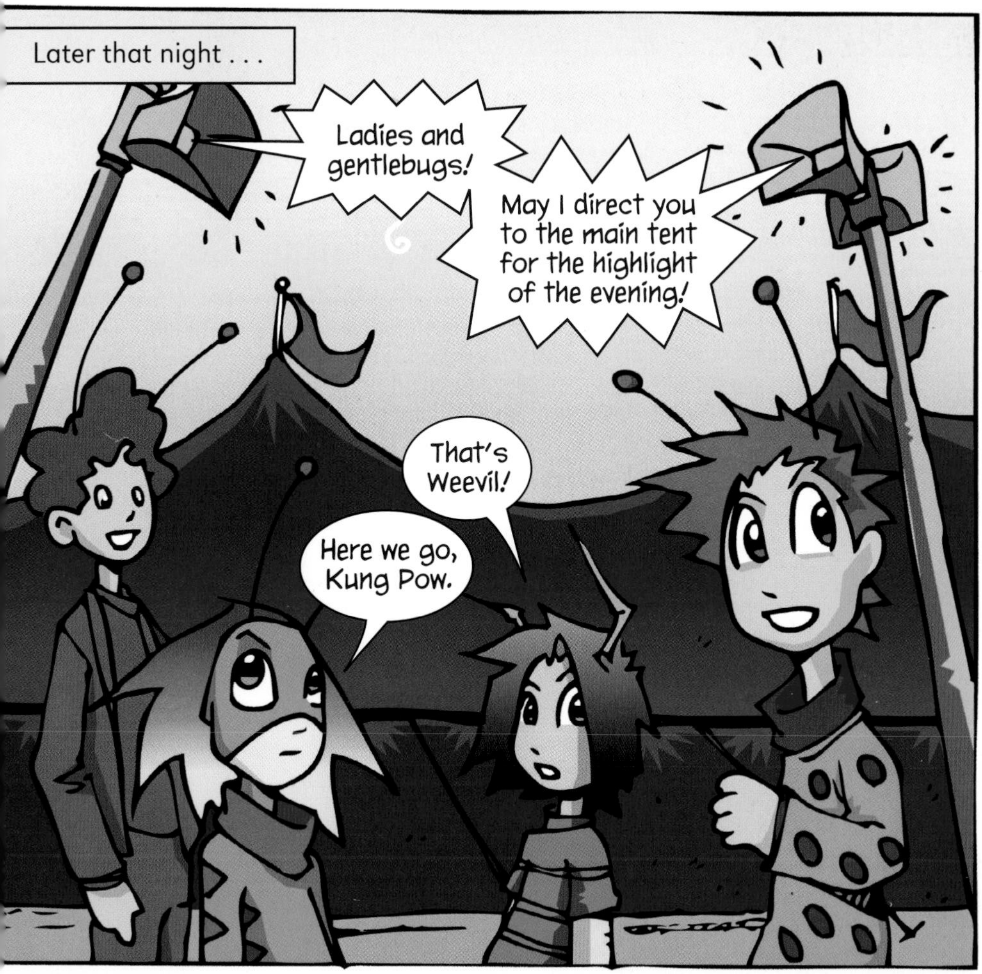
Later that night . . .
Ladies and gentlebugs!
May I direct you to the main tent for the highlight of the evening!
That's Weevil!
Here we go, Kung Pow.

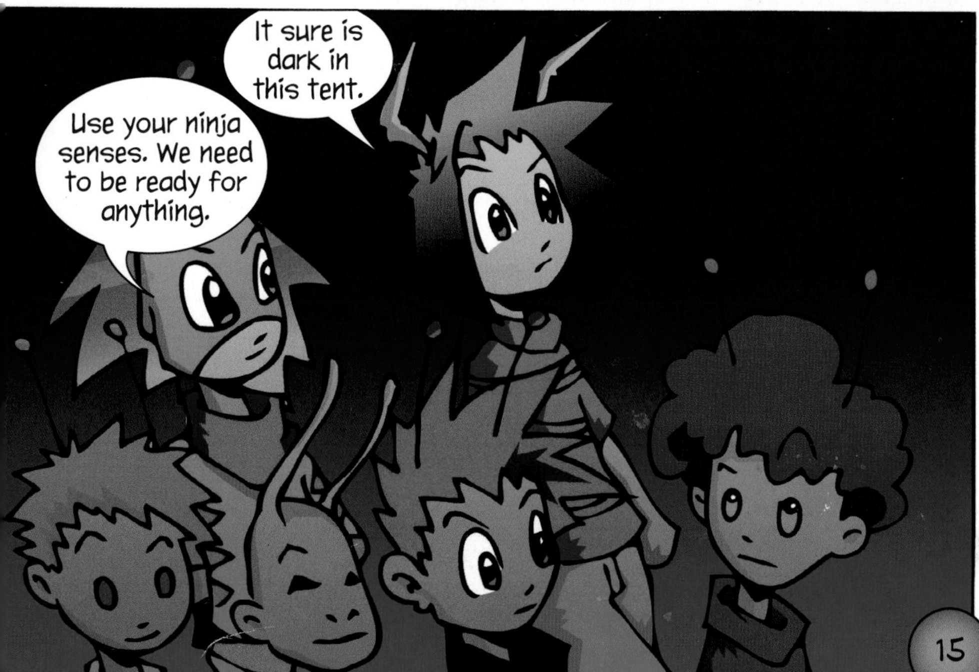
It sure is dark in this tent.
Use your ninja senses. We need to be ready for anything.

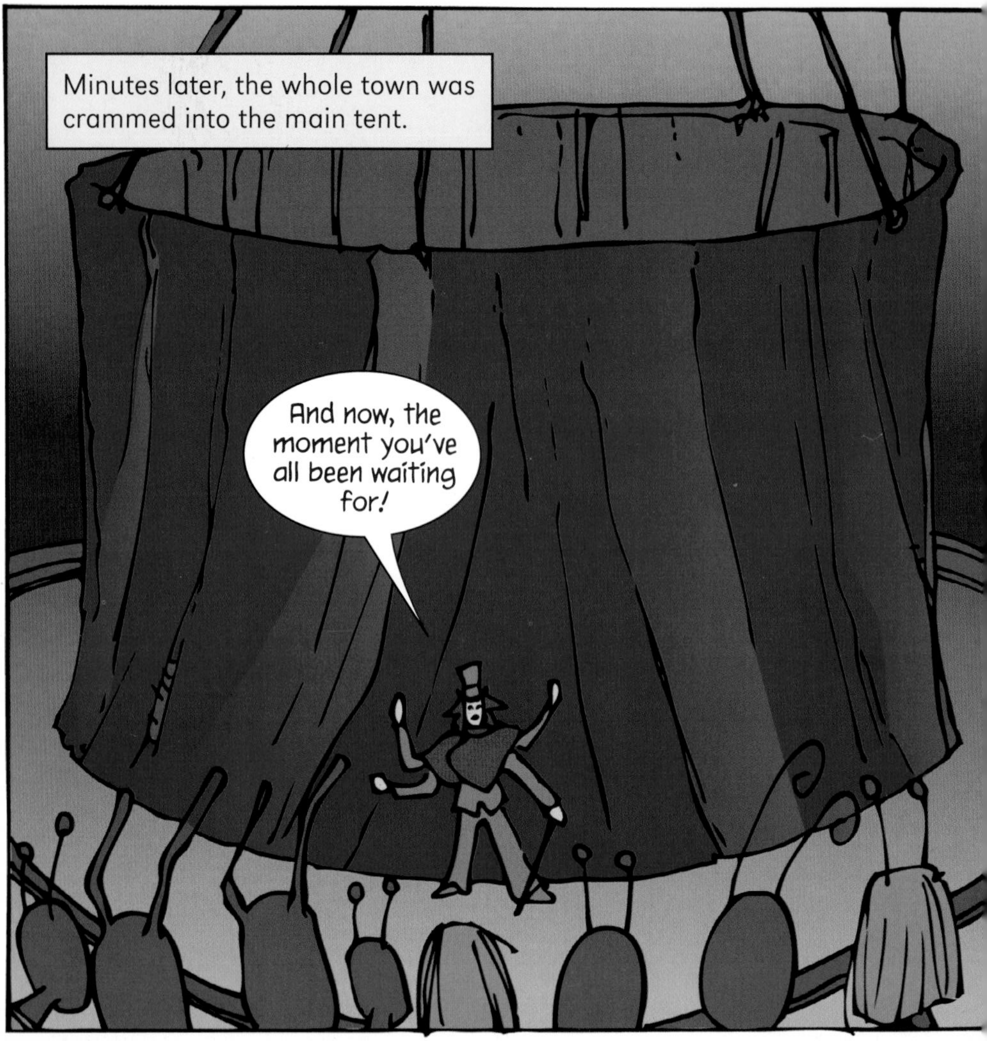
Minutes later, the whole town was crammed into the main tent.
And now, the moment you've all been waiting for!

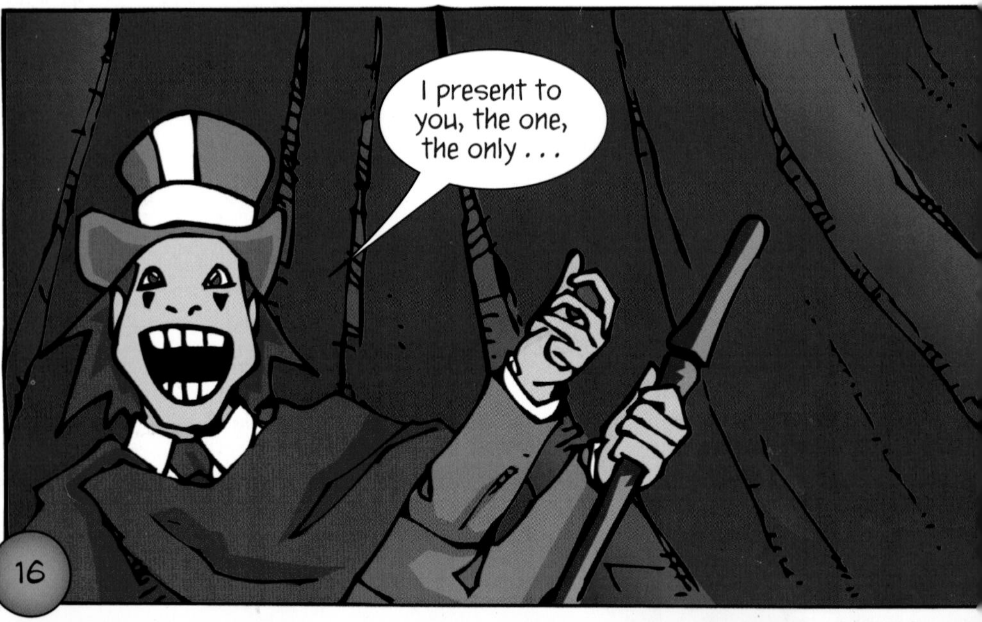
I present to you, the one, the only . . .

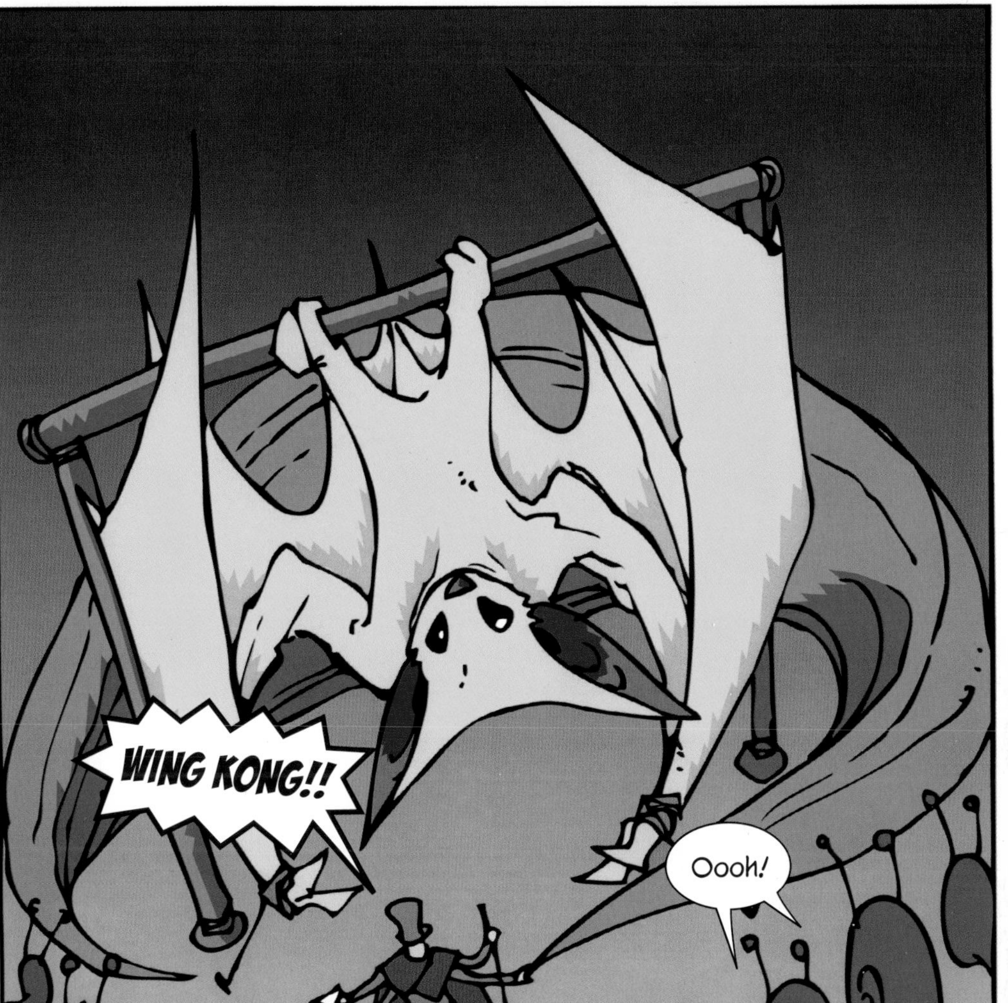
WING KONG!!
Oooh!

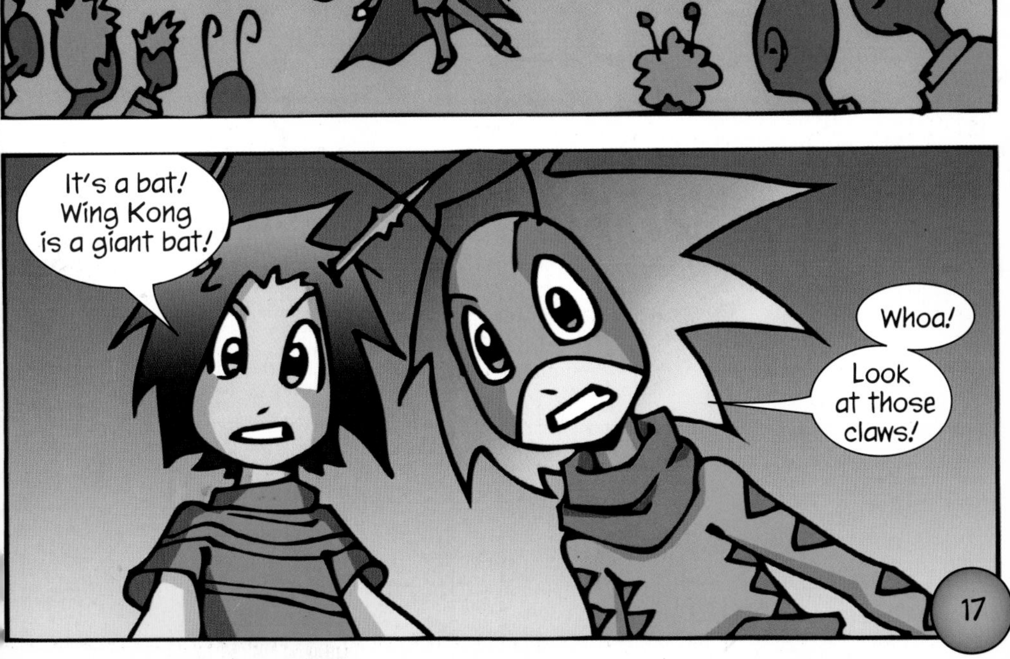
It's a bat! Wing Kong is a giant bat!
Whoa!
Look at those claws!

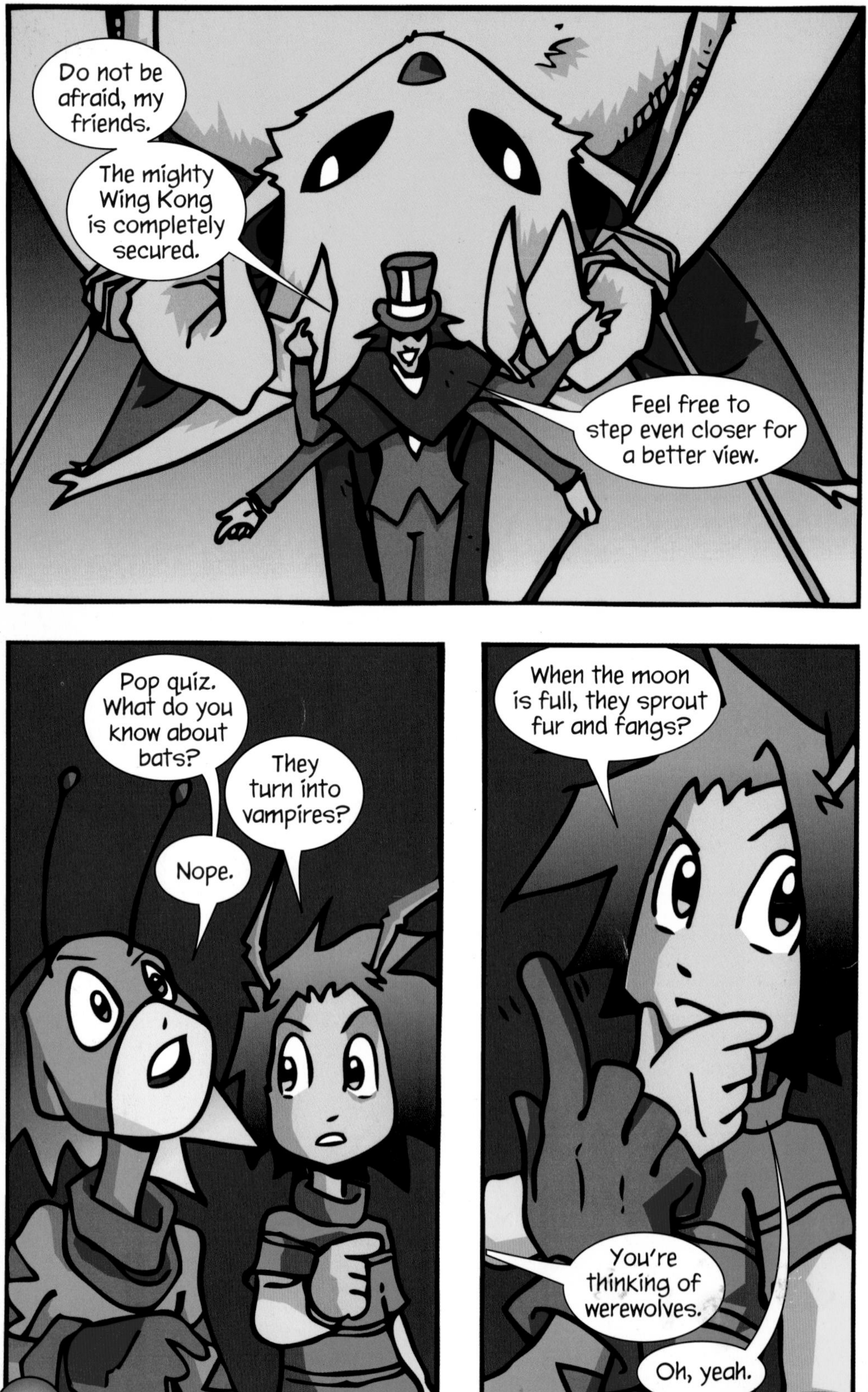
Do not be afraid, my friends.
The mighty Wing Kong is completely secured.
Feel free to step even closer for a better view.
Pop quiz. What do you know about bats?
They turn into vampires?
Nope.
When the moon is full, they sprout fur and fangs?
You're thinking of werewolves.
Oh, yeah.

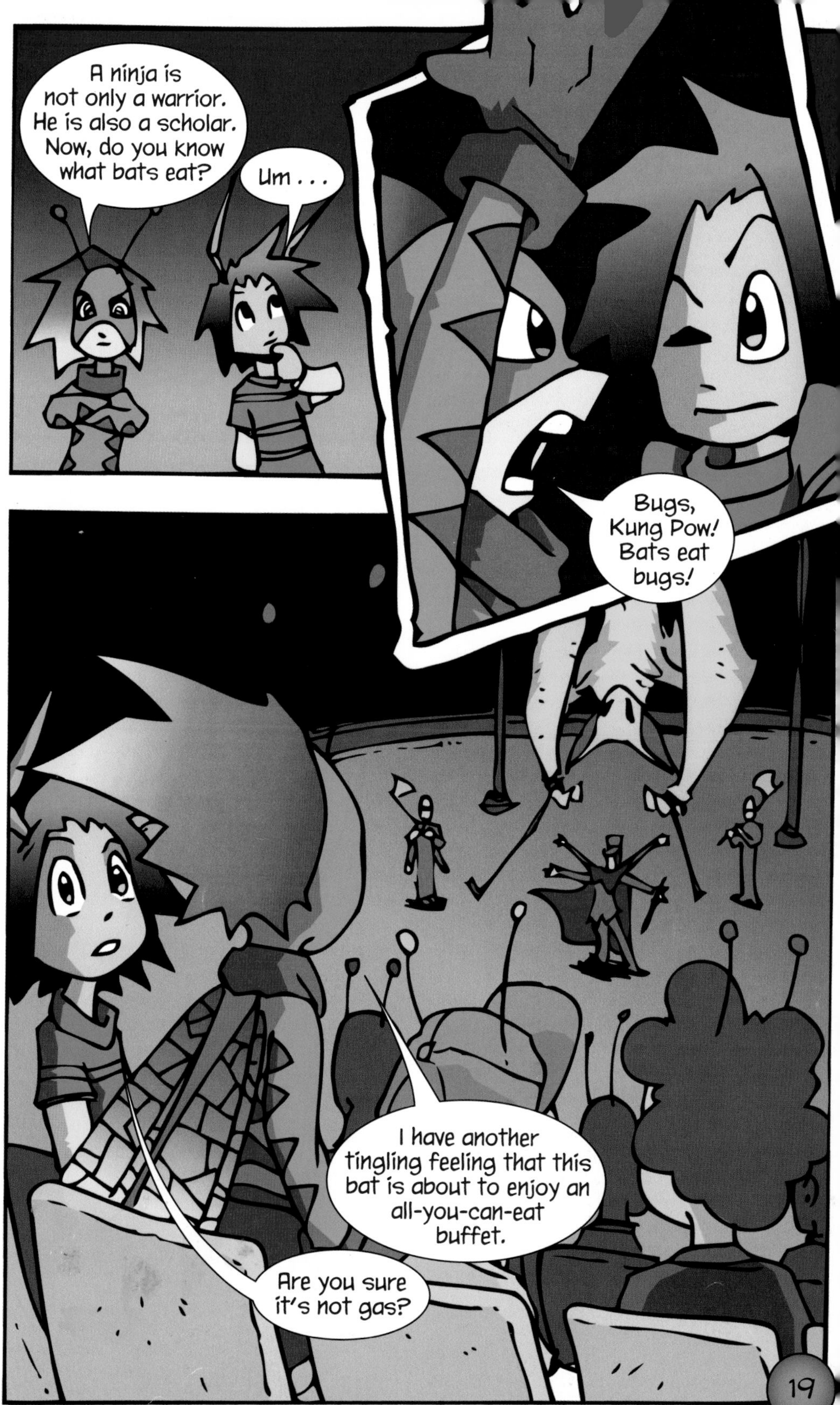
A ninja is not only a warrior. He is also a scholar. Now, do you know what bats eat?
Um . . .
Bugs, Kung Pow! Bats eat bugs!
I have another tingling feeling that this bat is about to enjoy an all-you-can-eat buffet.
Are you sure it's not gas?

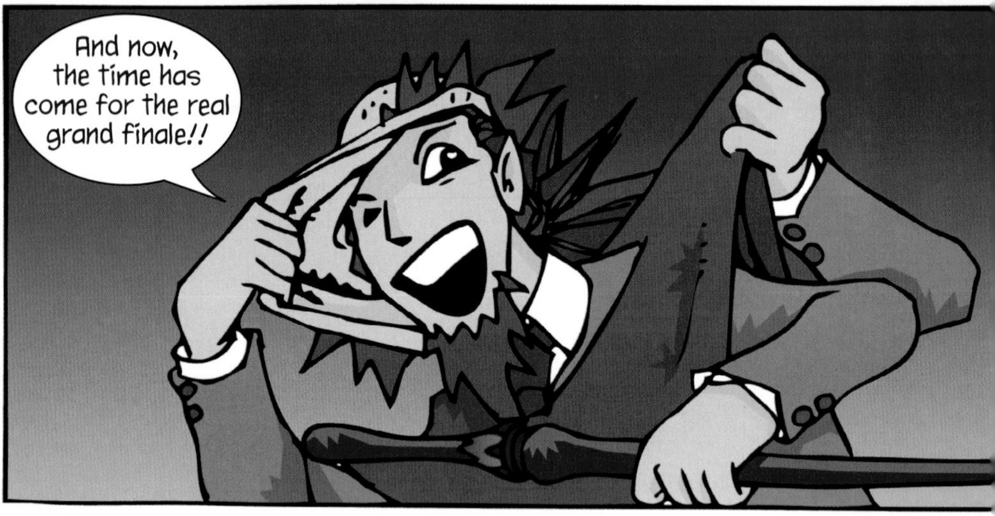
And now, the time has come for the real grand finale!!

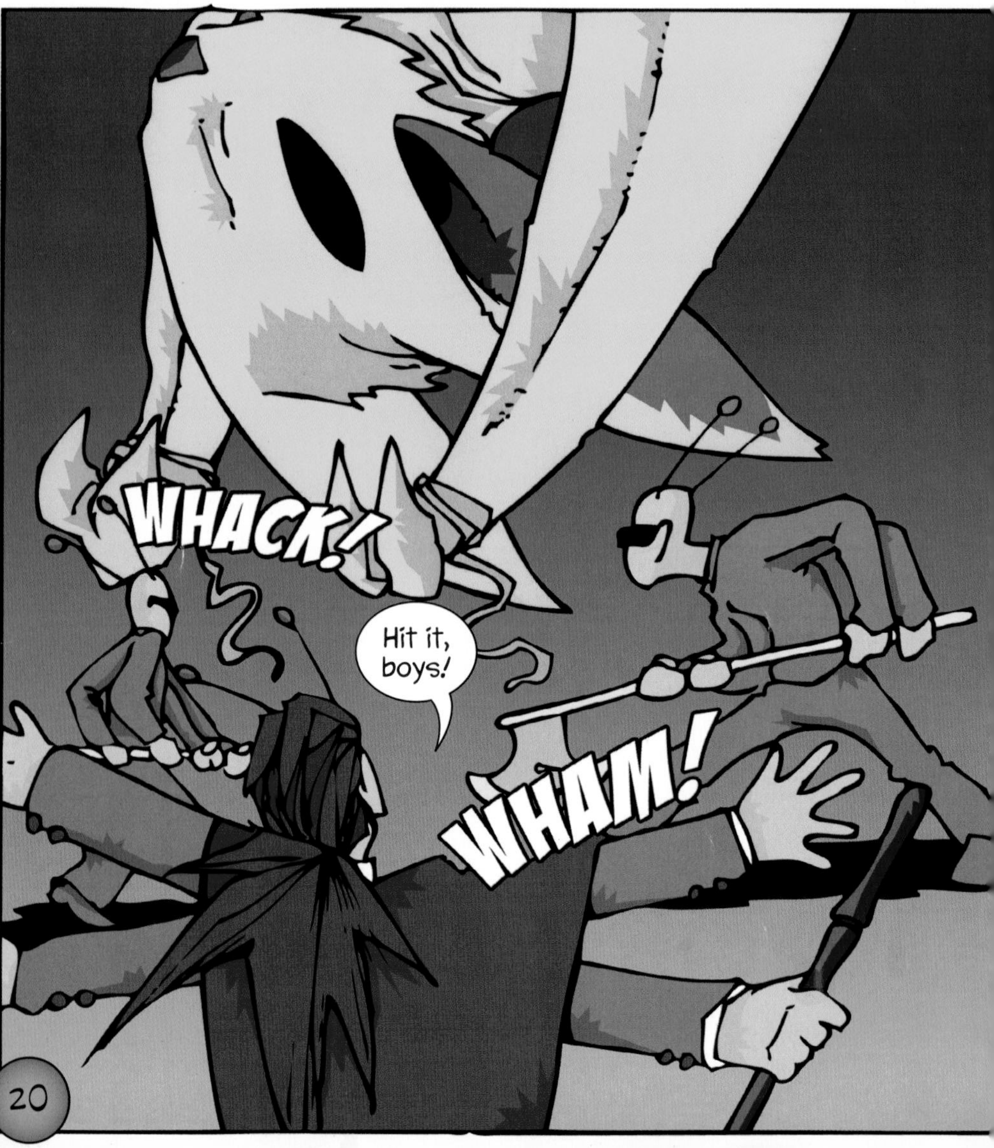
WHACK!
Hit it, boys!
WHAM!

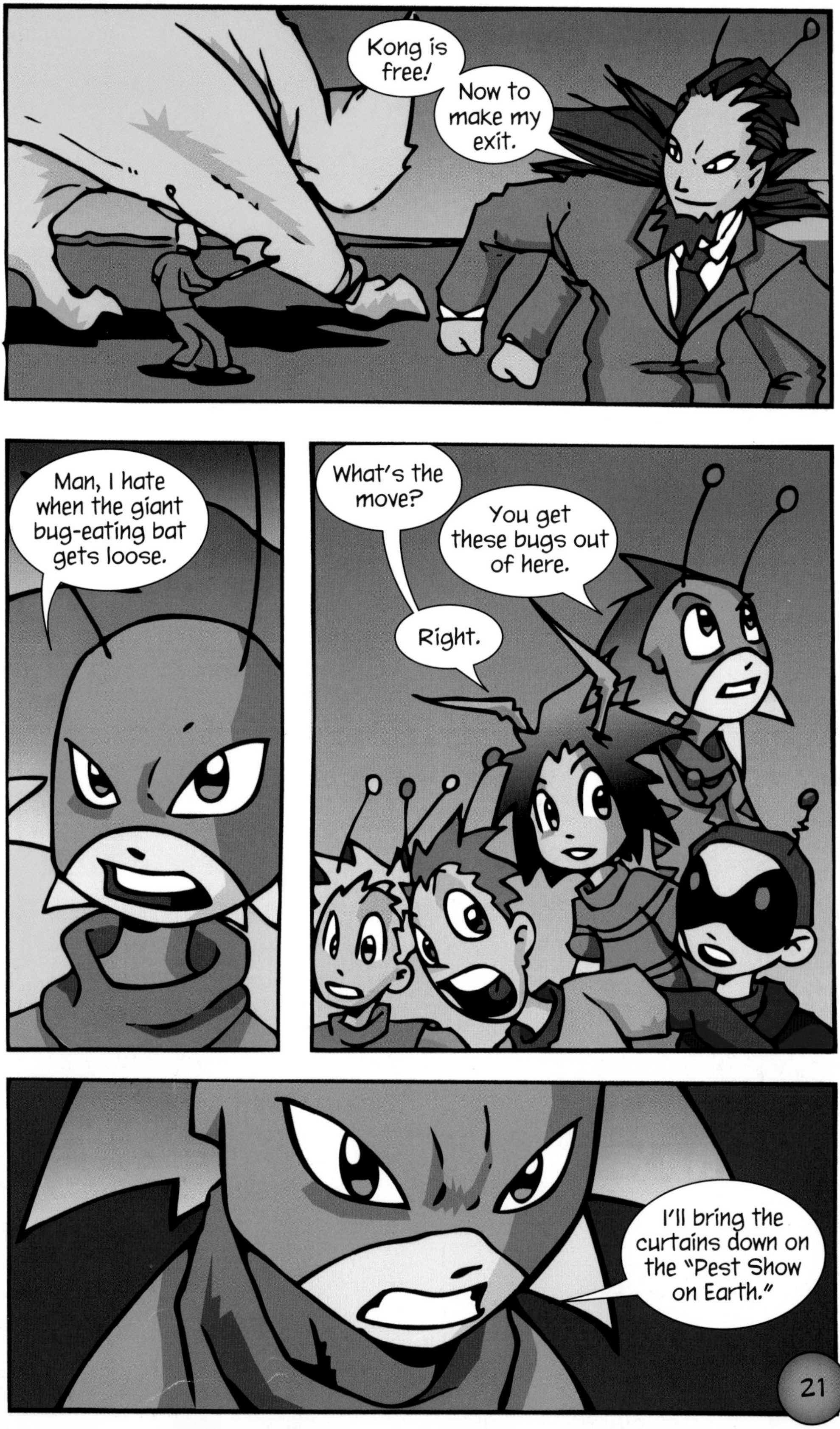
Kong is free!
Now to make my exit.
Man, I hate when the giant bug-eating bat gets loose.
What's the move?
You get these bugs out of here.
Right.
I'll bring the curtains down on the "Pest Show on Earth."

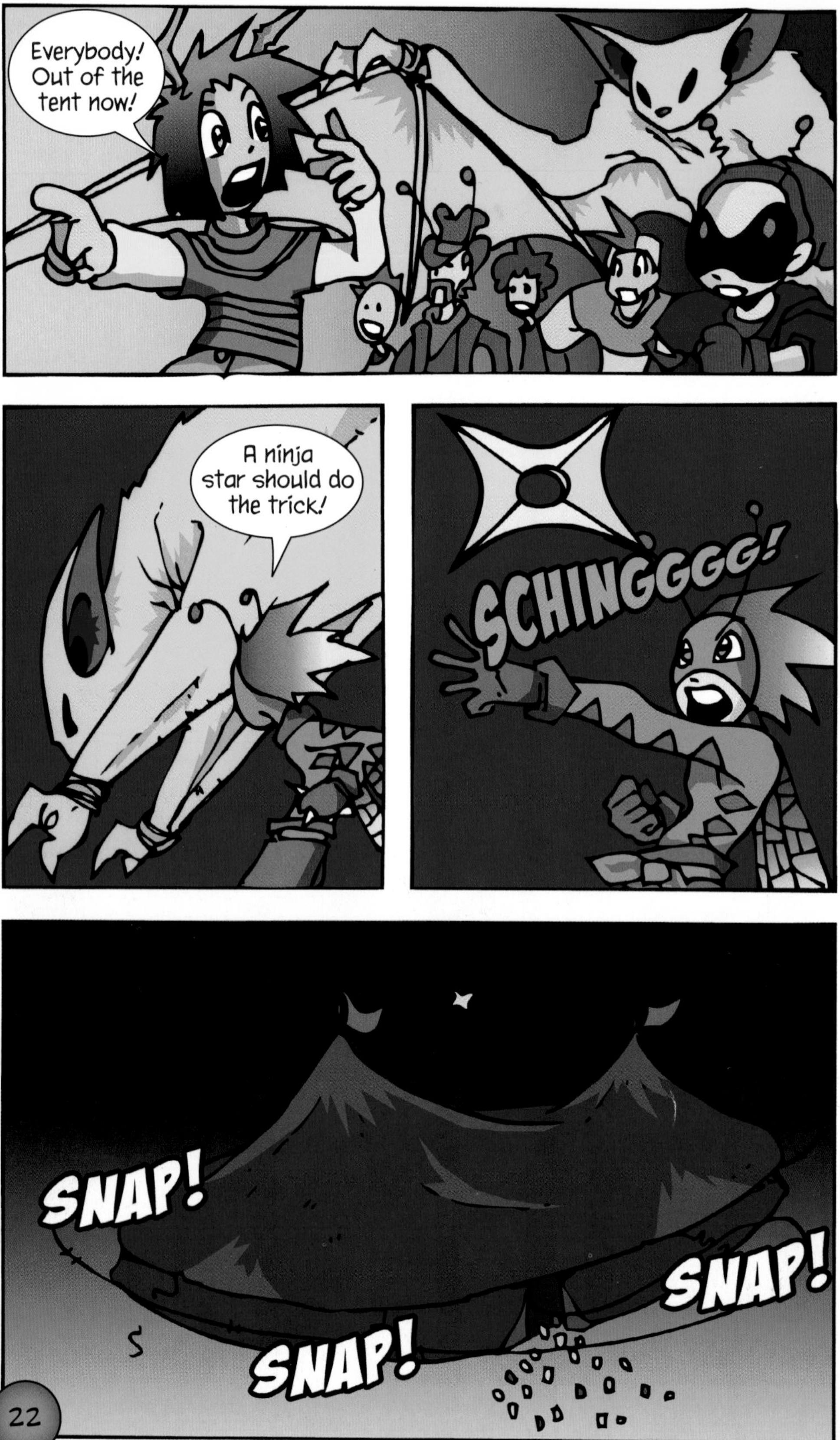
Everybody! Out of the tent now!
A ninja star should do the trick!
SCHINGGGG!
SNAP!
SNAP!
SNAP!

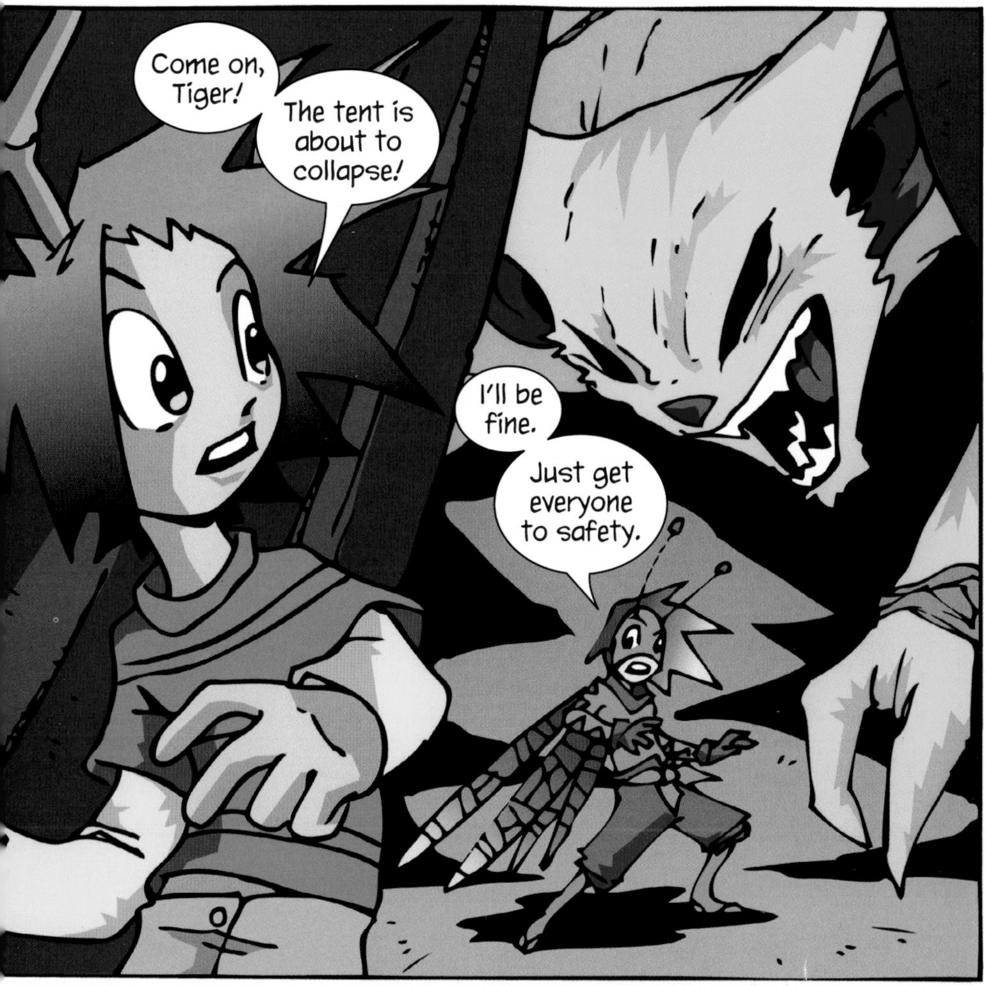
Come on, Tiger!
The tent is about to collapse!
I'll be fine.
Just get everyone to safety.

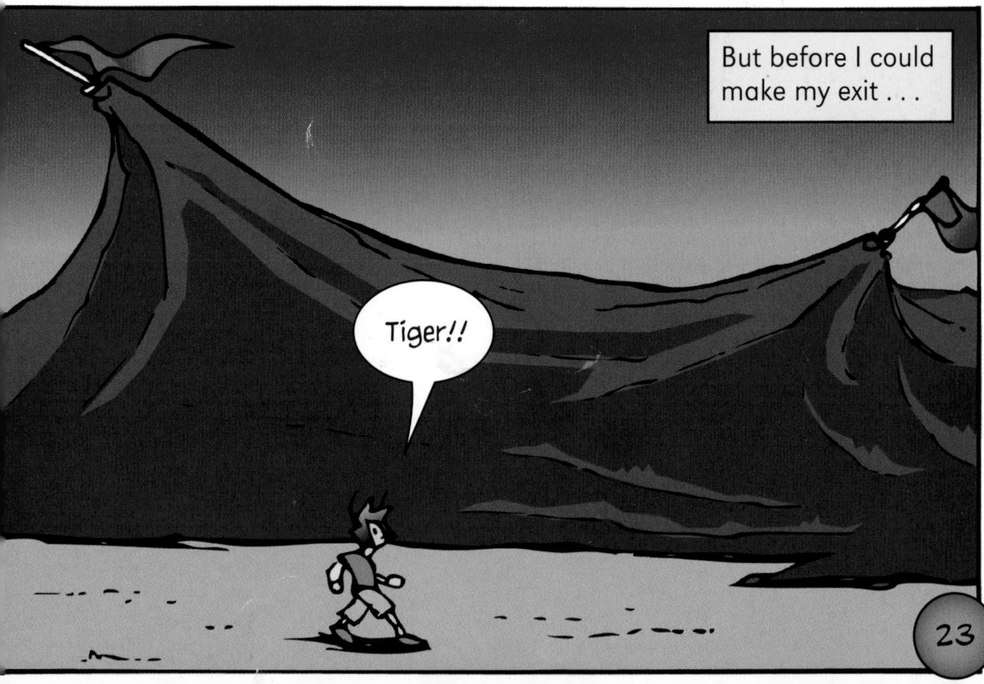
But before I could make my exit . . .
Tiger!!

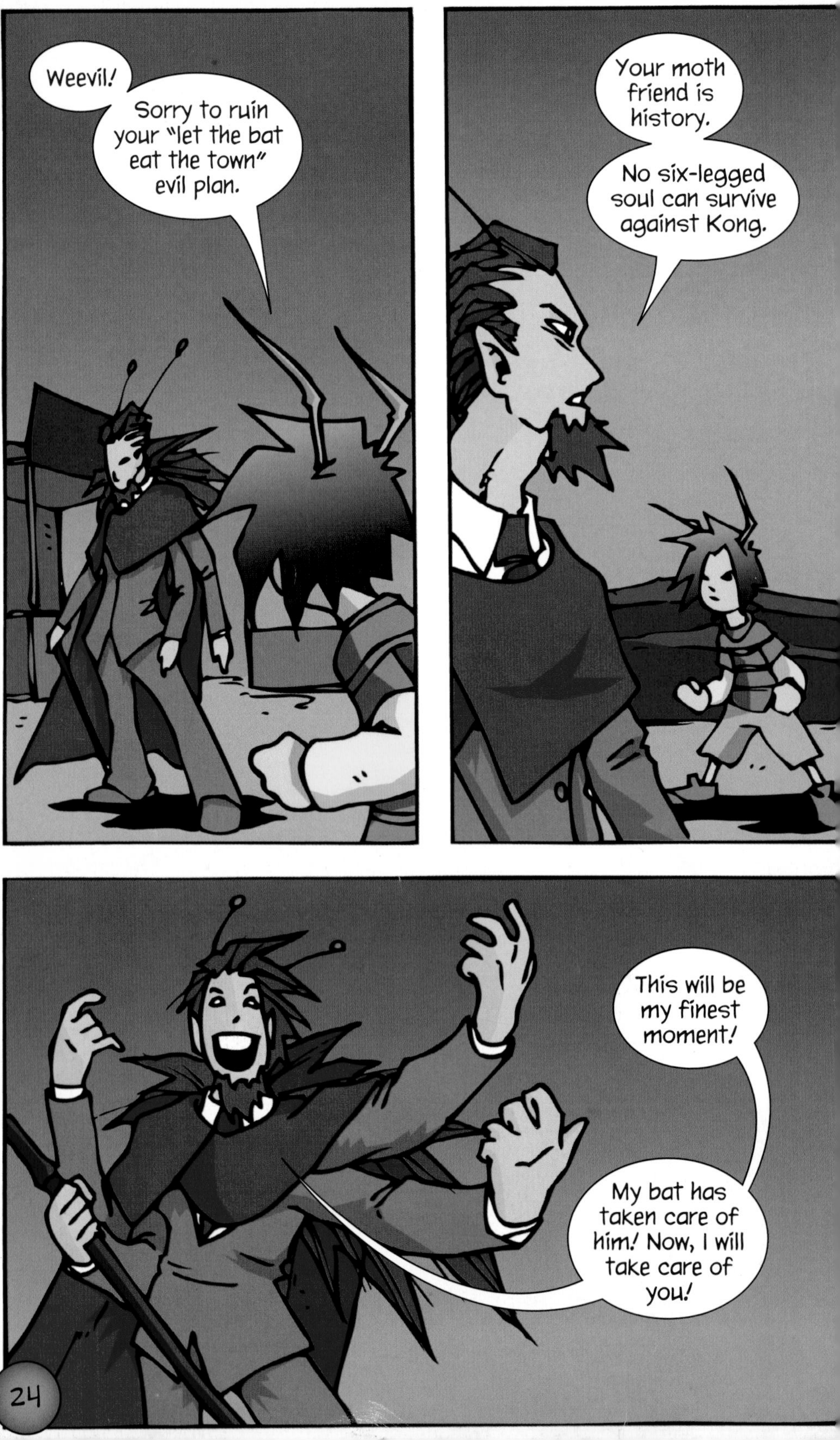

Weevil!
Sorry to ruin your "let the bat eat the town" evil plan.
Your moth friend is history.
No six-legged soul can survive against Kong.
This will be my finest moment!
My bat has taken care of him! Now, I will take care of you!

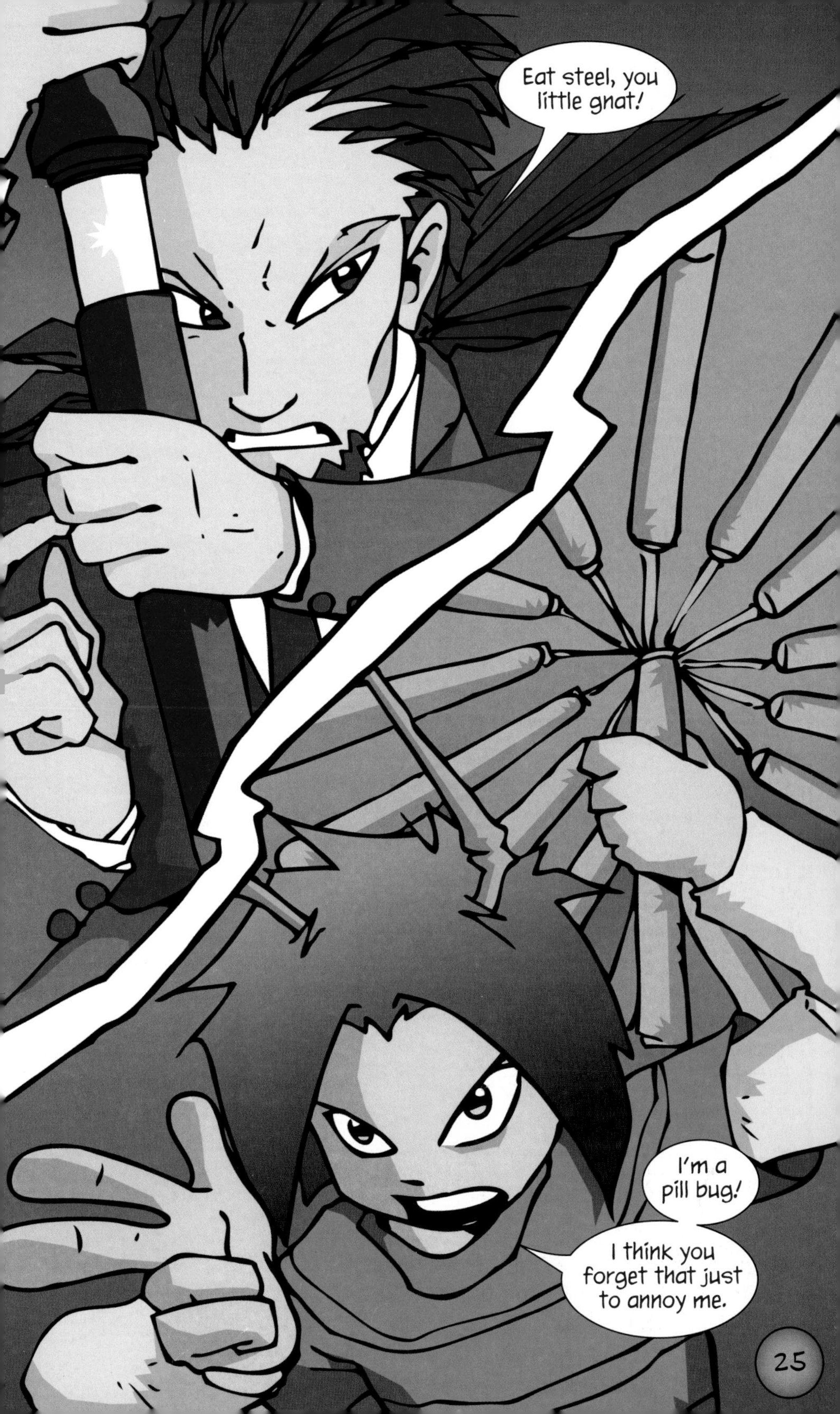
Eat steel, you little gnat!
I'm a pill bug!
I think you forget that just to annoy me.

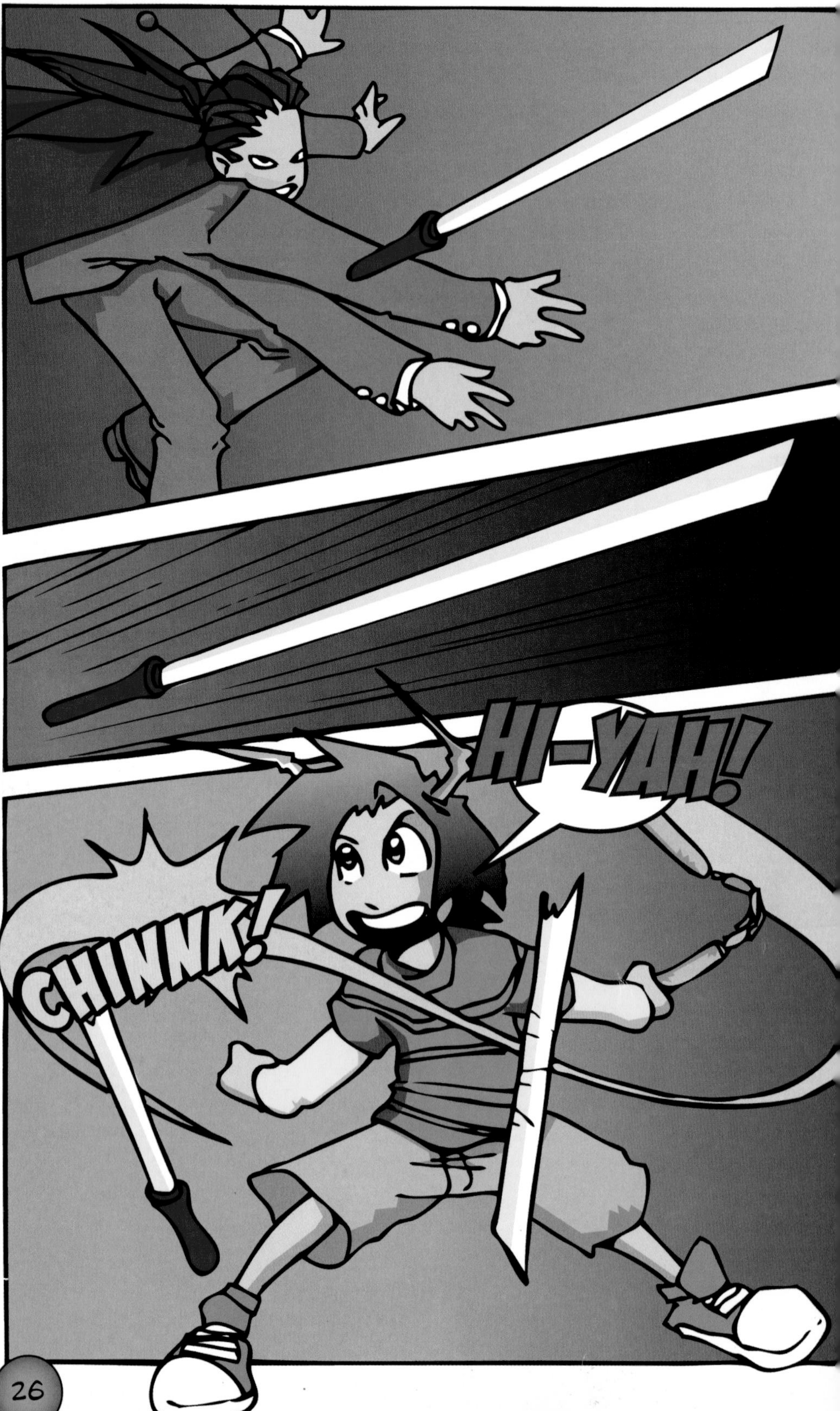
HI-YAH!
CHINNK!

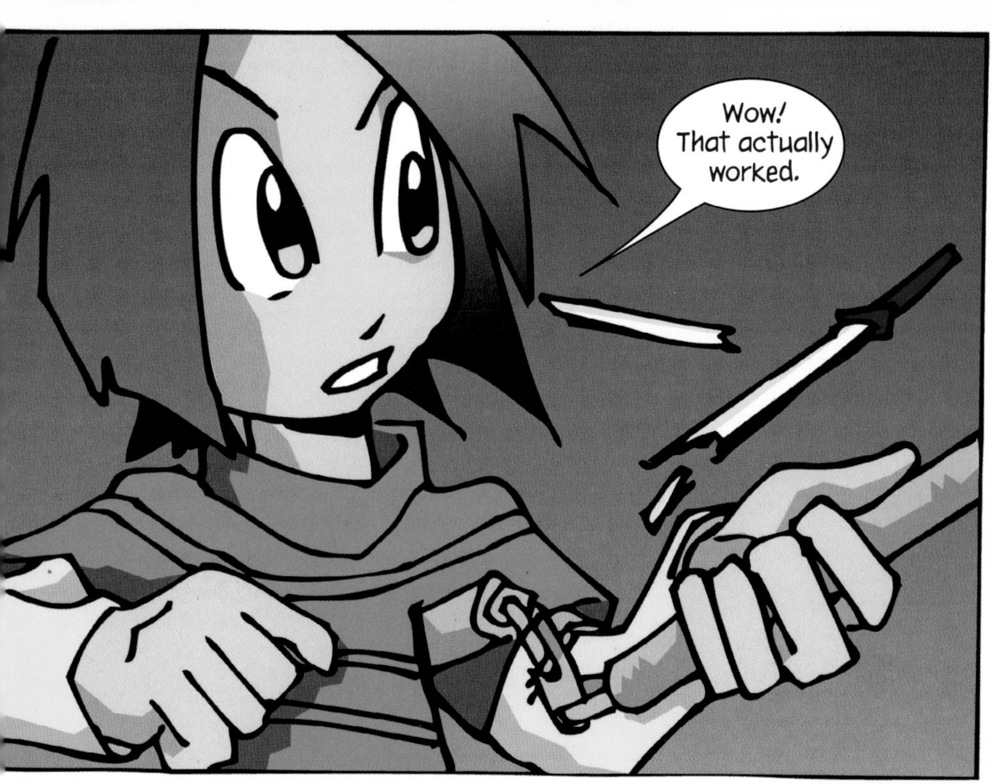
Wow! That actually worked.

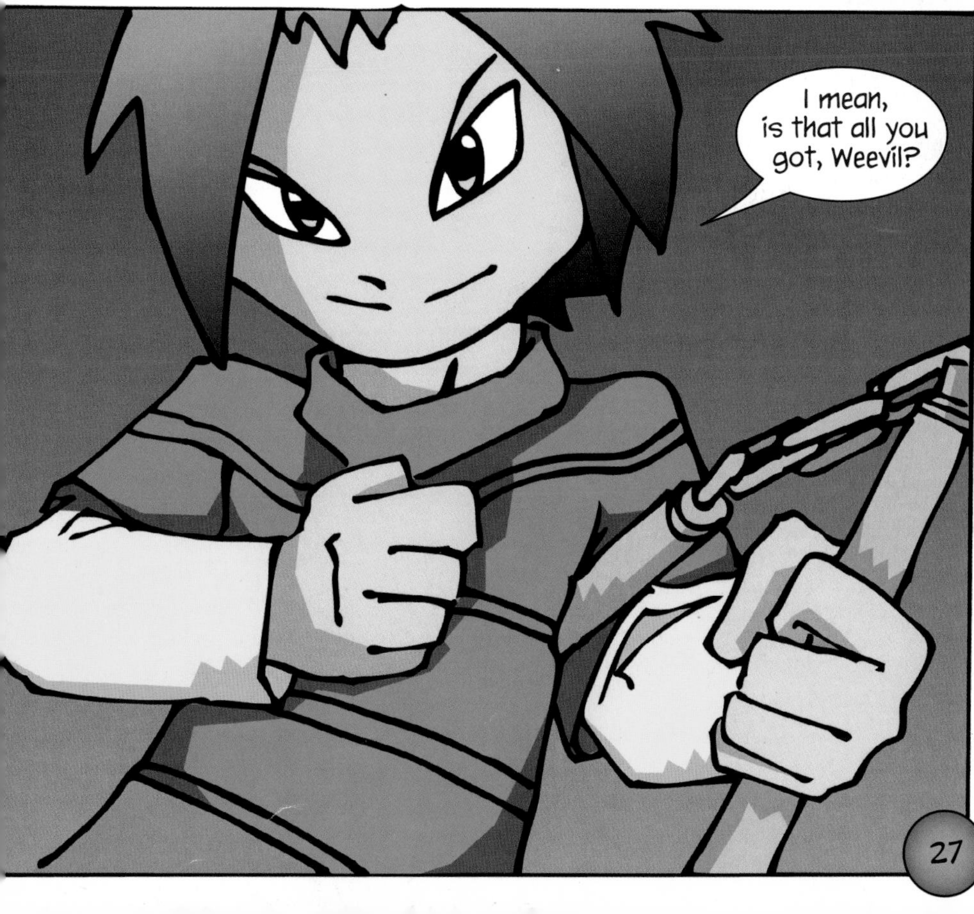
I mean, is that all you got, Weevil?

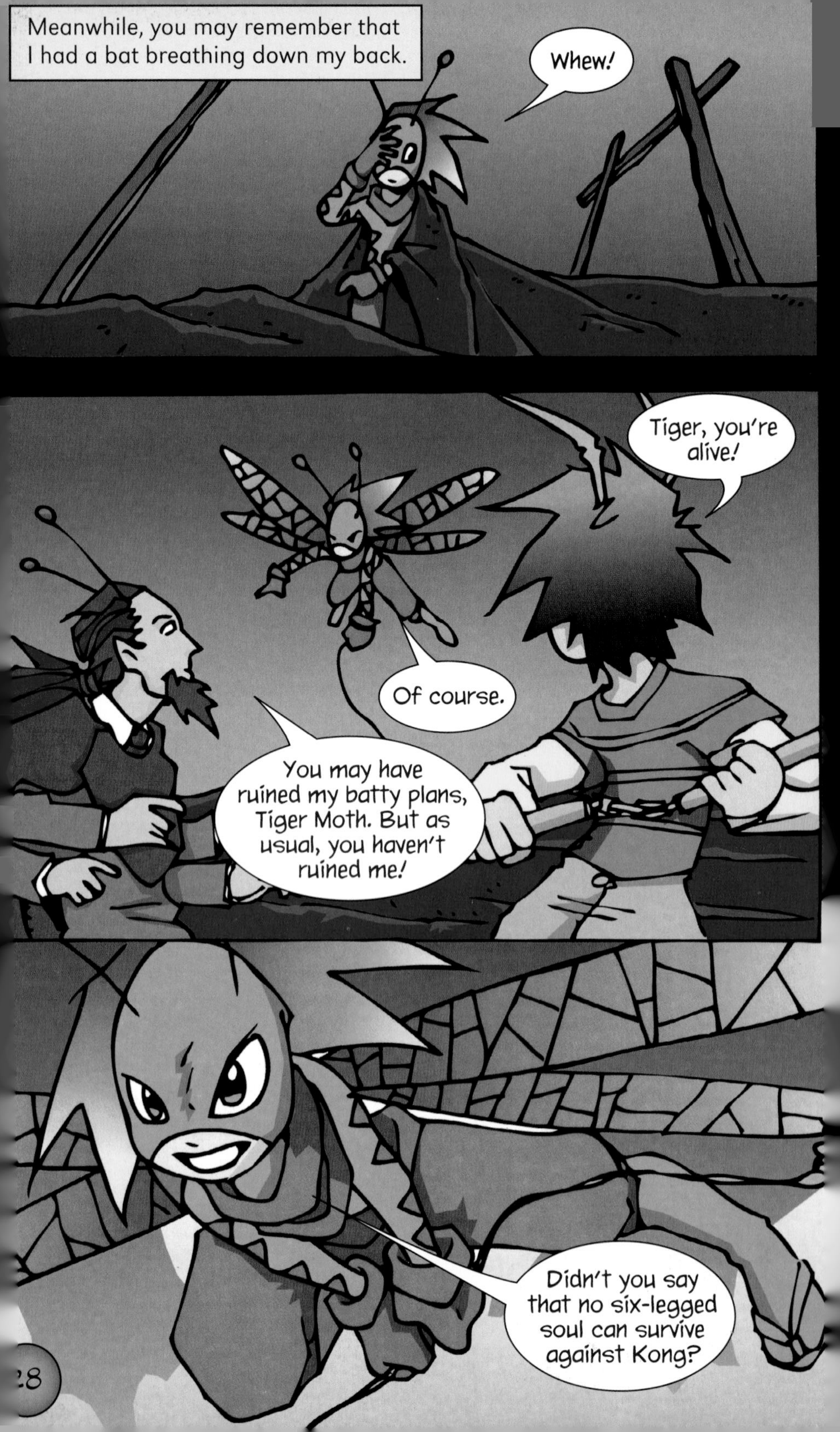

Meanwhile, you may remember that I had a bat breathing down my back.
Whew!
Tiger, you're alive!
Of course.
You may have ruined my batty plans, Tiger Moth. But as usual, you haven't ruined me!
Didn't you say that no six-legged soul can survive against Kong?

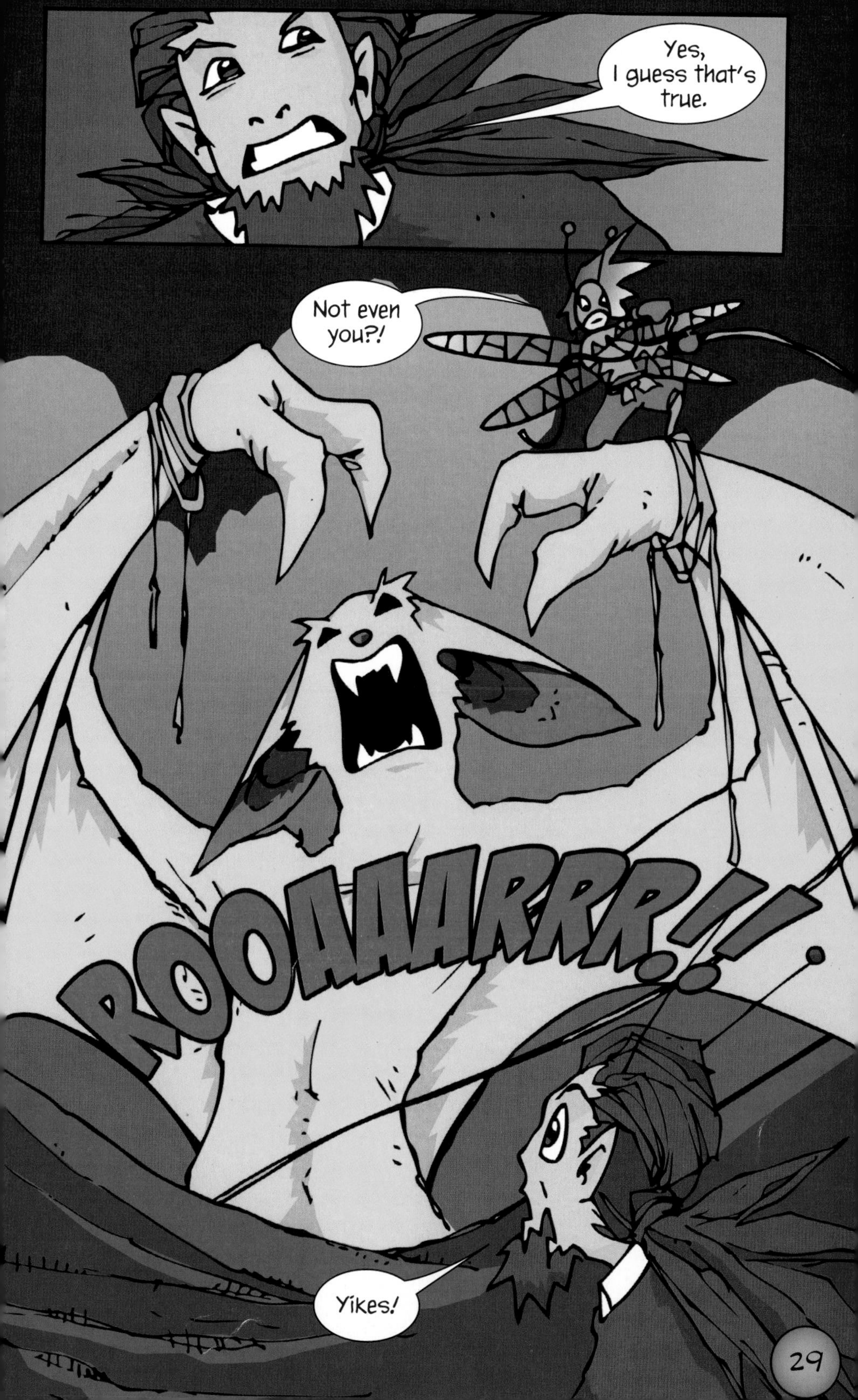
Yes, I guess that's true.
Not even you?!
ROOAAARRRR!!!
Yikes!

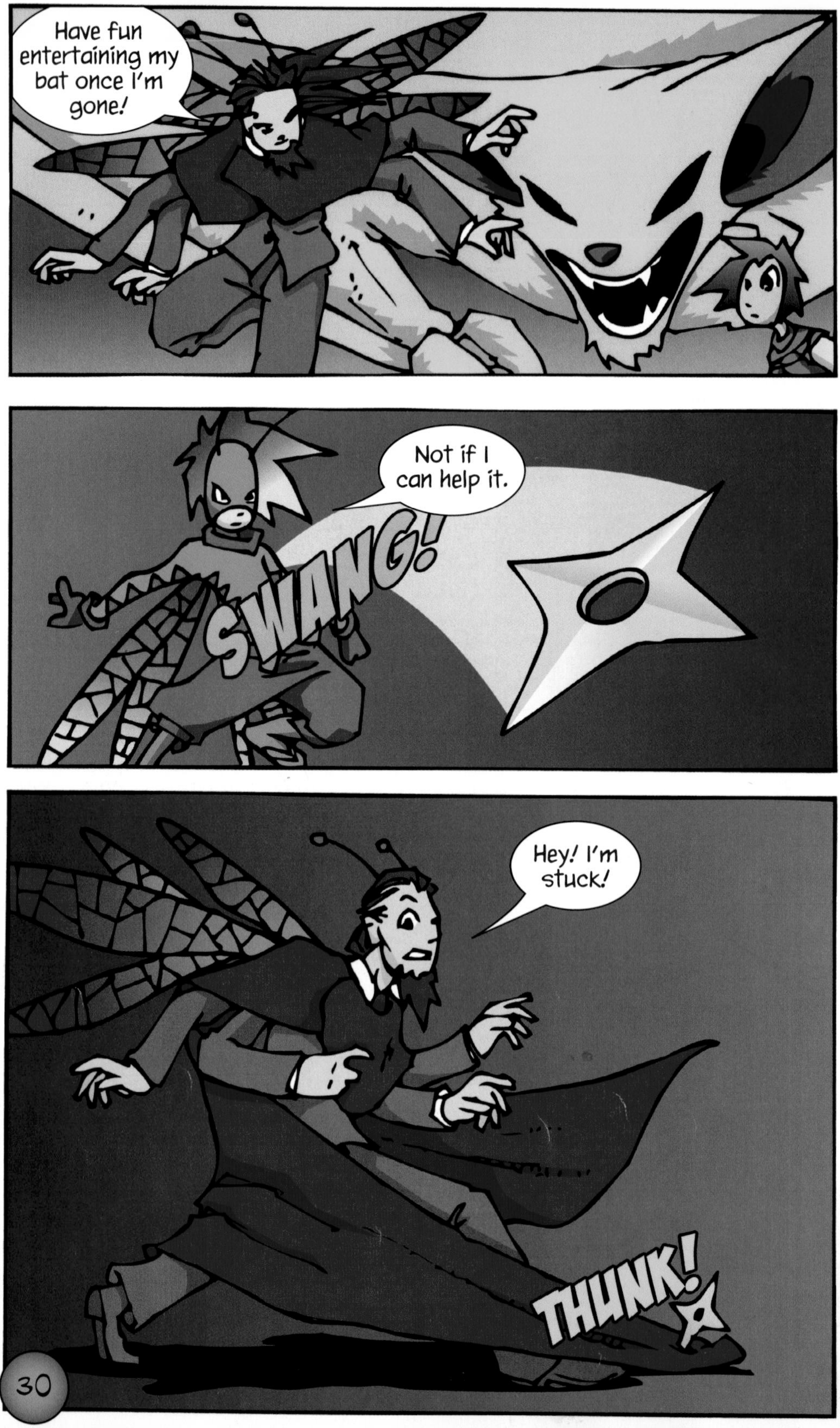
Have fun entertaining my bat once I'm gone!
Not if I can help it.
SWANG!
Hey! I'm stuck!
THUNK!

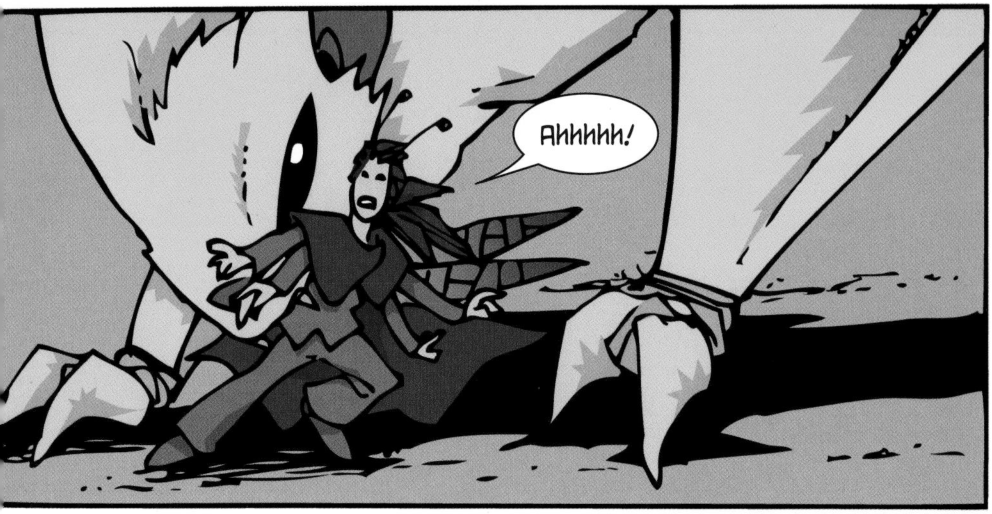
Ahhhhh!

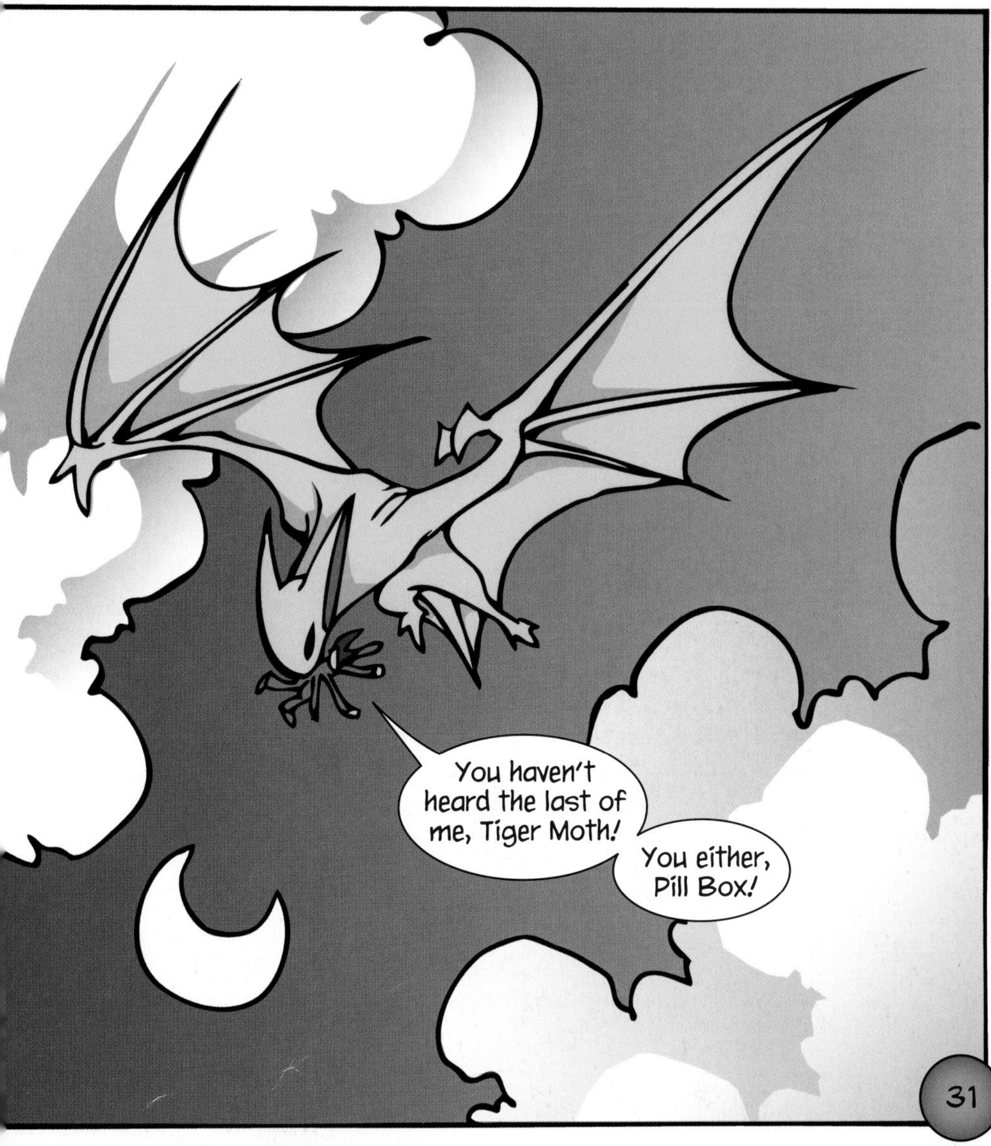
You haven't heard the last of me, Tiger Moth!
You either, Pill Box!

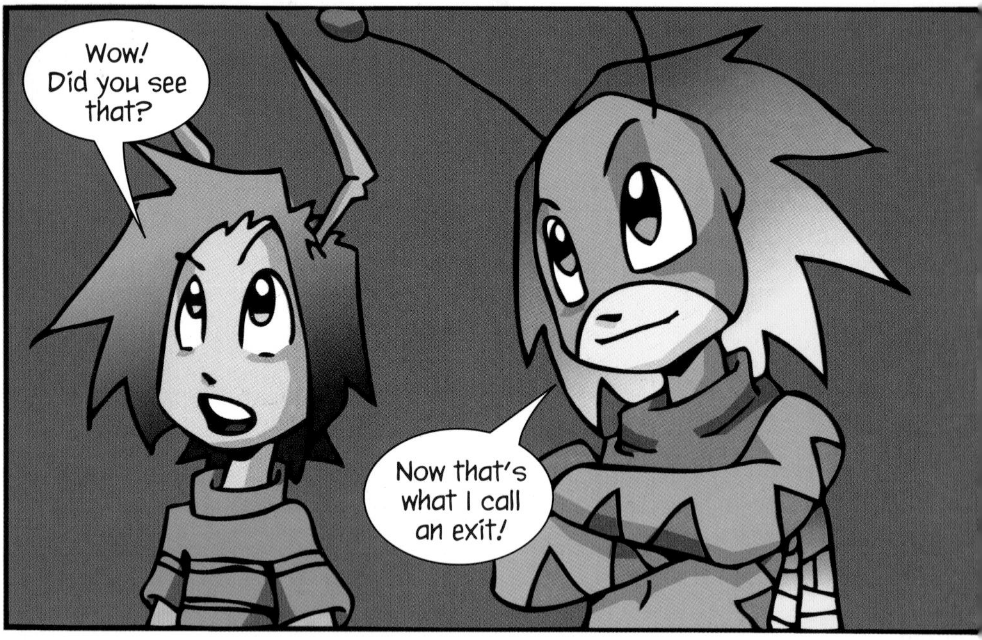
Wow! Did you see that?
Now that's what I call an exit!

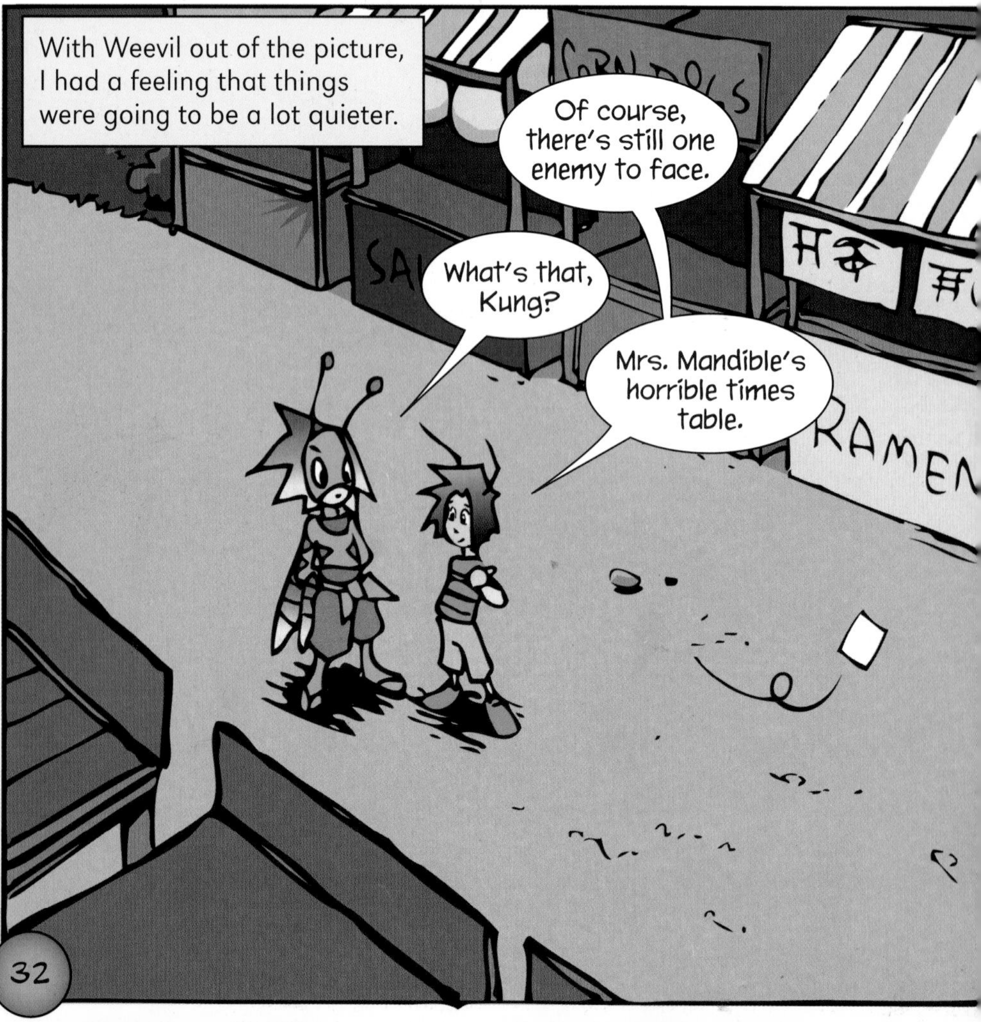
With Weevil out of the picture, I had a feeling that things were going to be a lot quieter.
Of course, there's still one enemy to face.
What's that, Kung?
Mrs. Mandible's horrible times table.
RAMEN

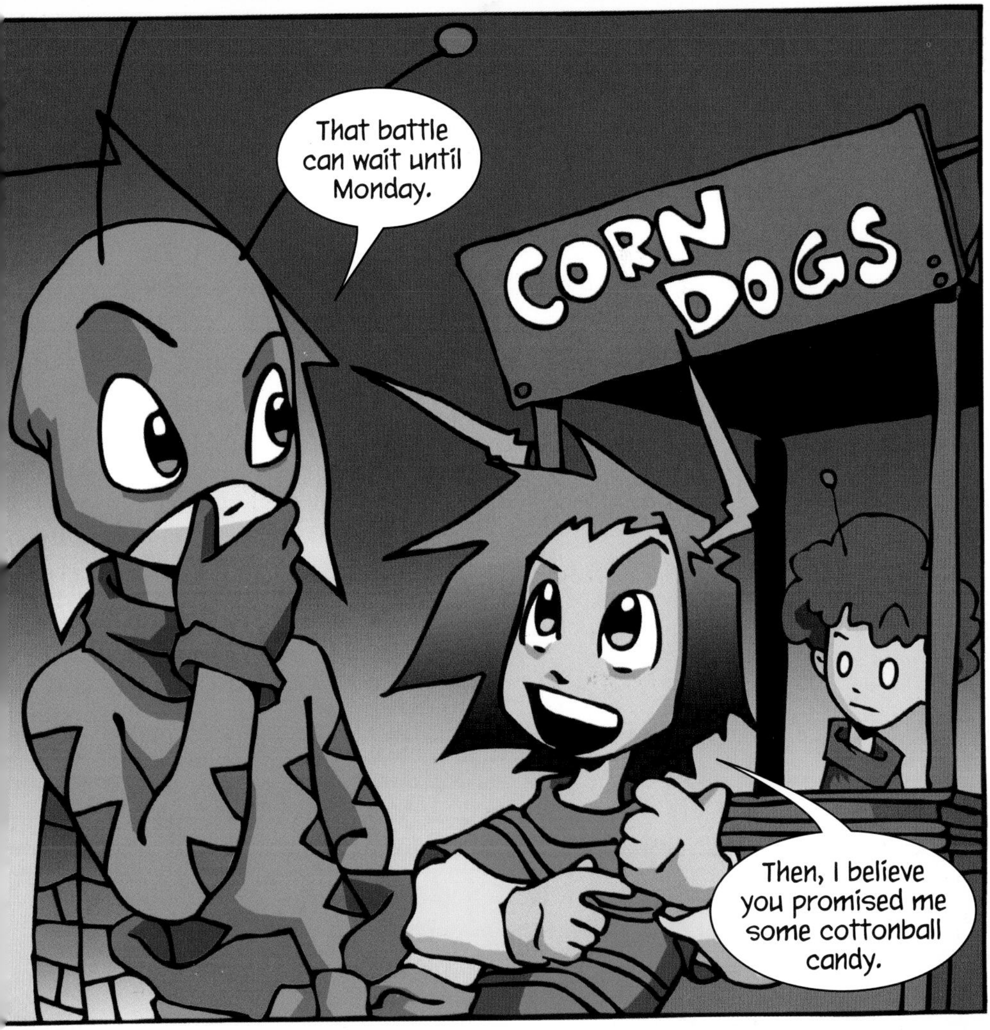
That battle can wait until Monday.
CORN DOGS
Then, I believe you promised me some cottonball candy.

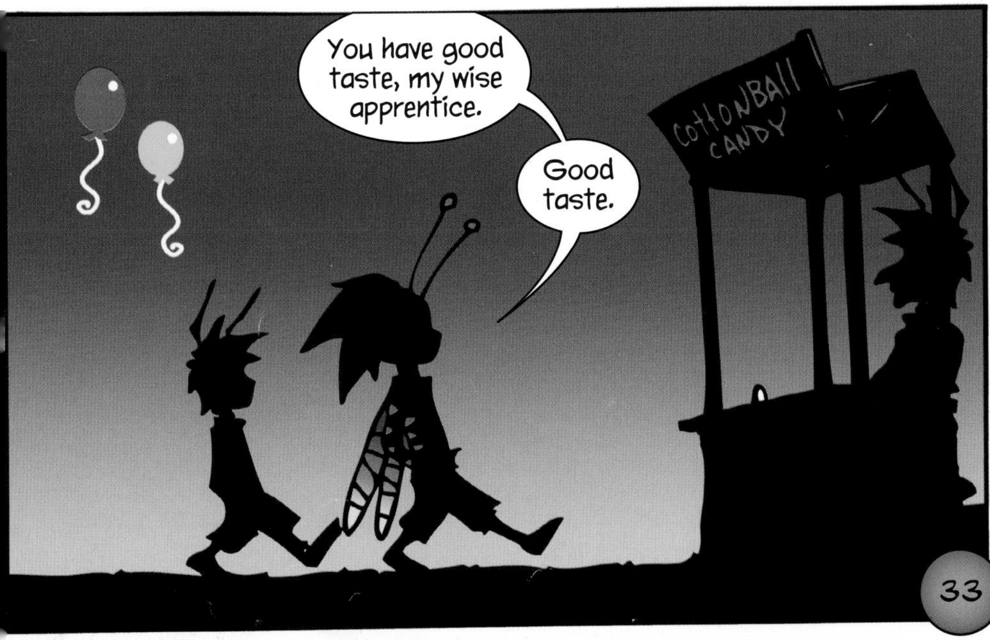
You have good taste, my wise apprentice.
Good taste.
COTTONBALL CANDY

About the Author

Aaron Reynolds loves bugs and loves books, so Tiger Moth was a perfect blend of both. Reynolds is the author of several great books for kids, including *Chicks and Salsa,* which *Publishers Weekly* called "a literary fandango." Reynolds had no idea what "fandango" meant. After looking it up in the dictionary, he learned the word means "playful and silly behavior." Reynolds hopes to write several more fandangos in the future. He lives near Chicago with his wife, two kids, and four insect-obsessed cats.

About the Illustrator

Erik Lervold was born in Puerto Rico, a small island in the Caribbean, and has been a professional painter. Deciding that he wanted to be a full-time artist, he moved to Florida, New York, Chicago, Duluth, and finally Minneapolis. He attended the Minneapolis College of Art and Design, majored in Comic Art, and graduated in 2004. Erik teaches classes in libraries in the Minneapolis area, and has taught art in the Minnesota Children's Museum. He loves the color green and has a bunch of really big goggles. He also loves sandwiches. If you want him to be your friend, bring him a roast beef sandwich and he will love you forever.

Glossary

apprentice (uh-PREN-tiss)—a young person that learns a skill from a more experienced person. This definition can work for bugs as well.

buffet (buf-AY)—a meal where guests serve themselves from many choices of foods laid out on a table

disguise (diss-GIZE)—something worn to hide a person or object's true identity; a mask is a type of disguise

exoskeleton (eks-oh-SKEL-uht-uhn)—the bony shell covering the outside of some insects

finale (fuh-NAL-ee)—the last part of a show

mothball (MOTH-bahl)—something used to keep pesky moths away from clothing

ringmaster (RING-mass-tuhr)—the person in charge of a circus. Weevil pretended to be a ringmaster, but really he's just an evil dude.

secured (si-KYOORD)—completely locked up with no chance of escape

shish-kebabbed (SHISH-kuh-bobd)—to be treated like a shish kebab, or a piece of meat or vegetable cooked on a skewer

soul (SOLE)—another word for person, or in this case, insect

villain (VIL-uhn)—an evil person . . . or evil bug

More About Traveling Shows

People have enjoyed traveling carnivals, circuses, and other festivals for centuries. During the Middle Ages, about 1,000 to 1,500 years ago, European villagers were entertained by **minstrels** (MIN-struhlz). These performers often sang songs, acted out plays, or told stories.

During the 1500s, laws stopped minstrels from traveling from town to town. But these laws didn't stop the shows. Instead, performers set up permanent buildings for their acts in towns across Europe.

The circus arrived in the United States in the early 1800s. During this time, Americans often lived too far away to travel to town for entertainment. In 1825, J. Purdy Brown had the idea to make the circus building out of canvas instead of wood. The canvas tent could be carried and set up closer to the customers.

Many early American circuses moved their equipment with horses and wagons. These shows could only travel about 20 miles a day. In 1872, Phineas Taylor Barnum started one of the first circuses to travel by train. They could reach more cities and more people.

In 1881, P. T. Barnum and James Anthony Bailey joined together and created the Barnum & Bailey circus. They called their circus "The Greatest Show on Earth."

In 1893, one of today's most popular carnival rides was created, the first Ferris Wheel. Invented by George W. Ferris, the ride stood 264 feet tall and could carry 2,160 passengers at a time.

Traveling carnivals combined the acts found at a circus with the rides found at a fair. Carnivals also had a display of weird and strange objects or people. This display was known as the sideshow. Early sideshows included fire-eaters, two-headed cows, and sword swallowers.

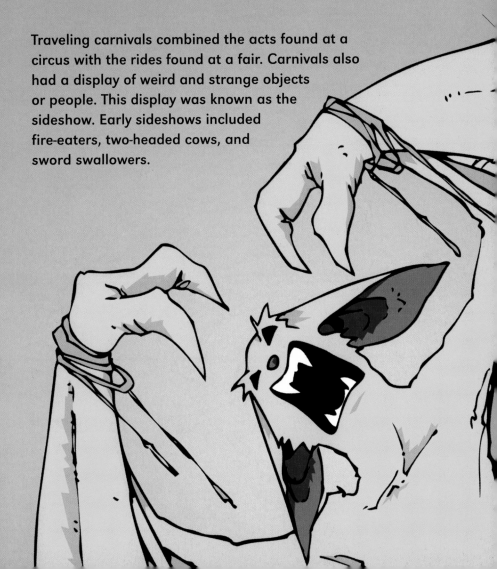

Discussion Questions

1. How does Kung Pow help out Tiger Moth in this story? Do you think Tiger could have defeated Weevil without his young apprentice? Explain your answer using examples from the story.

2. At the end of the story, Weevil is carried off by Wing Kong. Do you think this is the last time Tiger and Kung will have to face the evil bug? Why or why not?

3. This book was written and illustrated by two different people. If you had a choice, would you rather be an author or an illustrator? Explain your decision.

Writing Prompts

1. Except for the deadly Wing Kong, all of the characters in this story are bugs. Choose your favorite bug, and write your own story about it.

2. Where a story takes place is called the setting. The setting of this story is a carnival. Write a completely different adventure for Tiger Moth or Kung Pow using the exact same setting.

3. Have you ever been to a carnival, fair, or an amusement park? Describe your experience. What were your favorite rides, games, and foods?

Internet Sites

The book may be over, but the adventure is just beginning.

Do you want to read more about the subjects or ideas in this book? Want to play cool games or watch videos about the authors who write these books? Then go to FactHound. At *www.facthound.com*, you'll be able to do all that, and more. The FactHound website can also send you to other safe Internet sites.

Check it out!